Notting Hill Editions is an independent British publisher. The company was founded by Tom Kremer (1930–2017), champion of innovation and the man responsible for popularising the Rubik's Cube.

After a successful business career in toy invention Tom decided, at the age of eighty, to fulfil his passion for literature. In a fast-moving digital world Tom's aim was to revive the art of the essay, and to create exceptionally beautiful books that would be lingered over and cherished.

Hailed as 'the shape of things to come', the family-run press brings to print the most surprising thinkers of past and present. In an era of information-overload, these collectible pocket-size books distil ideas that linger in the mind.

James Rebanks is a farmer based in the Lake District, where his family have lived and worked for over six hundred years. His number one bestselling debut, *The Shepherd's Life*, won the Lake District Book of the Year, was shortlisted for the Wainwright and Ondaatje prizes, and has been translated into sixteen languages. His second book, *English Pastoral*, was also a top ten bestseller and was named the *Sunday Times* Nature Book of the Year. Heralded as a 'masterpiece' by the *New Statesman*, it was shortlisted for the Ondaatje Prize and longlisted for the Rathbones Folio Prize and the Orwell Prize for Political Writing. His latest book, *The Place of Tides*, set off the coast of Norway on a traditional eiderdown station, has been described as a 'modern classic'.

THE LAKE POETS

An Anthology

–

Introduced by
James Rebanks

nh Notting Hill Editions

Published in 2025
by Notting Hill Editions Ltd
Mirefoot, Burneside, Kendal LA8 9AB

EU Authorised Representative:
Easy Access System Europe
Mustamäe tee 50, 10621 Tallinn, Estonia
easproject.com
gpsr.requests@easproject.com

Series design by FLOK Design, Berlin, Germany
Cover design by Tom Etherington
Creative advisor: Dennis PAPHITIS

Typeset by CB Editions, London
Printed and bound by Imak Ofset, Istanbul, Turkey

Cover illustration 'Grasmere' by William Heaton Cooper R.I.
© copyright The Heaton Cooper Studio Ltd.

A CIP record for this book is available from the British Library

ISBN 978-1-912559-70-1

nottinghilleditions.com

There is one cottage in our dale,
In naught distinguished from the rest,
Save by a tuft of flourishing trees,
The shelter of that little nest.

The public road through Grasmere Vale
Winds close beside that cottage small,
And there 'tis hidden by the trees
That overhang the orchard wall.

You lose it there – its serpent line
Is lost in that close household grove;
A moment lost – and then it mounts
The craggy hills above.

– 'A Sketch' by Dorothy Wordsworth, *c.*1800–1803

Contents

– DOROTHY WORDSWORTH –

– SAMUEL TAYLOR COLERIDGE –

– ROBERT SOUTHEY –

– CHARLES LAMB –

JAMES REBANKS

– Introduction –

T hirty years after William Wordsworth died, the Reverend Hardwicke Drummond Rawnsley walked around Grasmere chatting to the locals in search of memories of the great poet. To a late nineteenth-century man of letters, Rawnsley, this must have seemed a rich seam to hack into because Wordsworth had by then been lionised as a giant of English poetry for several decades. So, who better to speak to about his legacy than the local working people who had sometimes featured in the poems?

There were a couple of problems with the endeavour: the locals had to be over forty years old to have overlapped, even in their childhood, with the elderly Wordsworth, and they had to have known who he was. Comically, Rawnsley struggled to find any memories of Wordsworth and his friends. It became almost funny because barely anyone he met seemed to give a damn about the greatest of the 'lake poets'. Rawnsley began to sense that there were two cultures in the Lake District, that of the locals, and that of the poets, and latterly their readers and scholars beyond the fells, and, in turn, of the visitors they inspired. These two cultures seemed to exist in parallel, but to be barely aware of each other.

Rawnsley speculated that as Wordsworth became a man of some importance he had stopped mingling much with shepherds and blacksmiths, and the rural people who had peopled his youth and his memories. He never went in their homes, or to the places where they worked, and only rarely talked to them. The few remembered conversations were of an oddball wandering about with his sister in tow, and what he'd said to the locals had seemed strange. He'd said they shouldn't white-wash their houses or that they had built their chimney in the wrong style. The people of Grasmere, it seems, didn't care much for Wordsworth, his writing, or his national fame.

I grew up in such a Lake District farming family, from a valley not far from those that Wordsworth wrote about. My dad would groan every bank holiday at the bad drivers on the roundabouts at Penrith as he went between our flocks of sheep and herds of cattle, and would ask rhetorically, '*Who in God's name encouraged all these idiots to come and clog up our roads?*'

I never heard the great poets' names – Wordsworth, Coleridge, Southey or Lamb – come from anyone's mouth, other than at school. I wondered what the fuss was about, these 'great dead white men' who pondered on clouds and daffodils, and mountain walks, and other chocolate-box things that no one I knew ever spoke of. I was, of course, determined to dislike them, these men who had somehow defined 'our' landscape for others.

As a young writer I wanted to seize my dad's frustration and run with it, tearing up the eighteenth- and nineteenth-century 'discovery of the Lake District' narrative. I'd tell everyone that this was the kind of 'cultural imperialism' that posh white people could no longer get away with anywhere else. I saw no reason why it should go unchallenged in our landscape. And I was in my thirties before I paid enough attention to their work to begin to see that I was not being entirely fair and that they represented a complex bundle of legacies, some of which benefitted and shaped my world and my family.

We tend to sift through literature for the age we live in, raiding it quite mercilessly for the bits we want, that comfort or speak to us, and ignore the rest. In the age of growing affluence, post World War II, with many families getting cars and paid holidays for the first time, we took the elements we wanted from the lake poets about being in nature, of escaping to the hills, and feeling it deeply like it was there for us. And we found a sense of ownership in Wordsworth's claim that the Lake District should belong to everyone with a heart to feel and eyes to see it. Millions of us could cultivate the right sensibility, owning whole landscapes simply by looking down on these valleys from the mountains and loving what we saw. Romanticism fed this. We could all be like Wordsworth and his friends.

My mum and her family made the trek up the M6 in their first car, in the 1960s, to enjoy this hard-won freedom, revelling in things that had been denied previous generations of her cotton-mill worker, often impoverished, undersized, Lancashire family. The freedom of the Romantics was a precious gift for them, an escape of the mind and the body from grimmer versions of the north. People like my mother's family wanted to walk across the fells, rest by the lake shore, or row a boat beneath the very same crags the young Wordsworth had. And they got an even more pared-back set of guides from Alfred Wainwright that cut the locals almost entirely out of the story in favour of the landscape that was now theirs, first as a National Park and later as a UNESCO World Heritage Site. I am a product of this Romantic culture too. Not just as a scribbler of words, but biologically. When my mum left home as a teenager, she came to work for the Outward Bound Trust in the Lakes, and then met my dad.

These poems have a complicated legacy – a tangle of threads, some good, some bad, some hard to judge. They taught the educated English (or perhaps the reading English) how to 'love nature', and shelves full of books about the same subject now attest to that. Though I'm not sure they taught the locals how to love their place; that seems a claim too far for me. They profoundly changed the way many people thought about beauty, not least our most rugged landscapes. They put the Lake District at the heart of the English literary imagination, turning it from an impoverished place associated with backwardness into our most cherished community. They also taught us what to do with our leisure time: no local ever walked fells while daydreaming, for leisure, in the deeper past. They also changed how we thought about childhood, as a time of innocence and formation before we are corrupted and numbed. And thank goodness Dororthy Wordsworth, in recent decades, has been rescued from being a footnote to her brother and is now seen as a writer of note, in addition to being a vital part of that friendship group and what they created. She now shines, with her own sensibility, judgment and vision.

By the time I was a kid in the 1980s, the romantic vision of the Lakes had been absorbed almost entirely into how British people (and many others around the globe) viewed landscapes. I sensed this romantic culture as a super-powerful thing when I was young, because it was.

A summer working in an office in London, as the century turned, killed off my last irritation about other people needing these things from our landscape. I soon wanted my own romantic escape back to the north after a few weeks of staring through glass and at concrete. I went home and began to read the lake poets properly for the first time, and books about them, and I found they had written about way more than daffodils, clouds and feelings. There had been a forgetting in the twentieth century about other themes of their work. The best poems came from their youthful radicalism meeting the hard-bitten realities of the north.

The poems and other writings are full of what can only be described as political beliefs, and radical ones for that time. They were writing against an increasingly industrial society, in which political power was held by the rich, landed and mercantile class, who often only served their own interests. They wrote about social injustices like extreme poverty, with poems full of references to beggars and other rural people who had fallen on hard times. We are left in no doubt that this clashes with any sense of social justice. In that respect they would prepare the way for more radical politics that led to the welfare state after World War II. To be intelligent and English was to see poverty, in the midst of a wealthy country, and feel outrage.

When these friends first came together it was against the backdrop of revolution in France and persecution of dissent by the nervous establishment of Britain. This group of youthful radicals attracted the attention of the authorities, who were aware of Wordsworth's time in revolutionary France. These were the punks of their day, daring to say and do things that made others uneasy. They came together like teenagers creating a modern band. William and Dorothy, Coleridge and Southey, all a bit broke, unemployed, and yet strangely confident that they had something to say that might matter, whilst being comfortably ensconced in other people's houses. They hung out alternating between moments of creation and youthful boredom. And from those conditions came their brilliance. They found a way to be radical in the most rural of places, Somerset and the Lake District.

We don't think of rural places and romantic poetry as being radical, but we should. And we need, perhaps, to read these poems with that tingle of excitement of knowing they once upset stuffy old people, who were scared of the change these writers threatened both on the page and in the world around them. The preface to Wordsworth and Coleridge's *Lyrical Ballads* lay down some beliefs that changed the course of literature: that ordinary life was a vital subject for poetry; that everyday language was appropriate for poets; that feelings were the stuff of poetry more than action or plot and that such feelings could be sought and found in places of tranquillity. It was a break with what came before, and the beginning of processes that are still unfolding to this day. I have learnt to be proud that this happened over the hills from me, a few short miles away.

These fells and valleys are not a tame place that exists to serve and soothe – they are their own place, with their own communities and their own values. This place I call home has again and again stood against what was being promoted by southern Britain, or the industrial north. And we need to push back again, because we live in an age of ecological collapse, climate change and the accumulation of wealth and power that would make anyone before this age gasp – a love of nature, or a questioning about how we live in it, are not peripheral issues: they are amongst the biggest issues we must now grapple with. Our effect on the planet is now so great, everywhere, and so all affecting that we have created a new epoch – the 'anthropocene'. We, in wealthy countries, now consume several times more resources per person than the planet can sustain, if everyone else did the same. An age in which billionaires become ever richer and more powerful, expanding their power and domination out in to space itself, and into our very bodies with AI. An age in which new industrial technologies threaten to overtake and overpower us, or, at the very least, demand energy and other resources on a scale no one has ever imagined. To pay attention to nature, to love it, and to think deeply about how we must live, is not the stuff of teenage daydreams – they are the great subjects of our age. I believe that we, in 'backwards' places, at the edge of things, often retain older values and ways of seeing. The edge is the place from which resistance is mounted. If that's improbable, remind yourself that every National Park, every protected piece of landscape on earth, owes a little something to these writers. They were among the first to dream that such a kind of 'ownership' was possible.

The best lines in the poems, for me, are those that give us glimpses of the people of the Lake District dales. People who were, too long, outside the pages of literature. The glimpses are sometimes frustrating, and of their time, but they are also exciting because a new way of seeing is being born. The scholars call it 'human ecology' – the study of traditional human communities as an interconnected part of their ecosystems.

If we are to escape our worst flaws, it will be by learning to live well in places again, with some humility. We need to think about that a lot more than we have done so far, looking for lessons from older ways of life that consumed less and got more of what sustained them, spiritually and culturally, from their natural surroundings. If we are to fight back to try and change the dominant narrative of our age then we must listen to the earth around us and see it, and our work in it, with clarity. This is what it means to be 'romantic'.

When Wordsworth wrote his *Guide to the Lakes*, in 1810, he described the valleys he knew as a 'perfect republic of shepherds and agriculturalists'. In his eyes, it was a community that had shaped a landscape, and had been shaped by it in turn. A people with attributes and values he admired, a model, with less hierarchy of wealth and class, for another kind of England. I believe something similar. The answers to our broken and corrupted age won't come from the centre, from the rich and powerful, or from business-as-usual, but they might come from the places and people at the edge, off the beaten track, from those least corrupted by our vices, and from our listening to them. We need the spirit in these poems, and a new even bolder version of it for our own age.

WILLIAM WORDSWORTH
(1770–1850)

One of Britain's most celebrated poets, William Wordsworth is known for his distinctive, lyrical style, inspired by the landscape of the Lake District where he spent much of his life. He was born in 1770 in Cockermouth, Cumbria, though his idyllic childhood was overshadowed by the death of his parents. After studying at St John's College, Cambridge, he travelled through France during the time of revolution and was greatly influenced by the drive for political justice. On his return, he was horrified to find that England had declared war on France. Reunited with his sister Dorothy Wordsworth, who had been separate from her brothers after their parents' deaths, the Wordsworths set up home in Alfoxden, Somerset, in 1796. The following year, they welcomed Samuel Taylor Coleridge as a guest, which marked the beginning of a prolific pairing of poetic and political minds. As a result of this friendship (and with insights from his sister, Dorothy), their book the *Lyrical Ballads* was published in 1798, now widely regarded as the cornerstone of Romanticism. On a walking tour back in his native Lake District, Wordsworth stumbled across a former pub in Grasmere, which – renamed Dove Cottage – became a home for him, Dorothy, his wife, Mary Hutchinson, and their children. A few years later, they moved to Rydal Mount near Rydal Water, also in the Lake District. In his later years, Wordsworth's political views shifted significantly, and by the time he accepted the honour of Poet Laureate in 1843, the radical Wordsworth had departed entirely.

– An Evening Walk (1793) –

Far from my dearest friend, 'tis mine to rove
Through bare grey dell, high wood, and pastoral
    cove;
Where Derwent rests, and listens to the roar
That stuns the tremulous cliffs of high Lodore;
Where peace to Grasmere's lonely island leads,
To willowy hedge-rows, and to emerald meads;
Leads to her bridge, rude church, and cottaged
    grounds,
Her rocky sheepwalks, and her woodland bounds;
Where, undisturbed by winds, Winander sleeps
'Mid clustering isles, and holly-sprinkled steeps;
Where twilight glens endear my Esthwaite's shore,
And memory of departed pleasures, more.
    Fair scenes, erewhile, I taught, a happy child,
The echoes of your rocks my carols wild:
The spirit sought not then, in cherished sadness,
A cloudy substitute for failing gladness,
In youth's keen eye the livelong day was bright,
The sun at morning, and the stars at night,
Alike, when first the bittern's hollow bill
Was heard, or woodcocks roamed the moonlight
    hill.
    In thoughtless gaiety I coursed the plain,
And hope itself was all I knew of pain;
For then, the inexperienced heart would beat
At times, while young Content forsook her seat,

And wild Impatience, pointing upward, showed,
Through passes yet unreached, a brighter road.
Alas! the idle tale of man is found
Depicted in the dial's moral round;
Hope with reflection blends her social rays
To gild the total tablet of his days;
Yet still, the sport of some malignant power,
He knows but from its shade the present hour.

 But why, ungrateful, dwell on idle pain?
To show what pleasures yet to me remain,
Say, will my Friend, with unreluctant ear,
The history of a poet's evening hear?

 When, in the south, the wan noon, brooding still,
Breathed a pale steam around the glaring hill,
And shades of deep-embattled clouds were seen,
Spotting the northern cliffs with lights between;
When crowding cattle, checked by rails that make
A fence far stretched into the shallow lake,
Lashed the cool water with their restless tails,
Or from high points of rock looked out for fanning
    gales:
When school-boys stretched their length upon the
    green;
And round the broad-spread oak, a glimmering
    scene,
In the rough fern-clad park, the herded deer
Shook the still-twinkling tail and glancing ear;
When horses in the sunburnt intake stood,
And vainly eyed below the tempting flood,

Or tracked the passenger, in mute distress,
With forward neck the closing gate to press –
Then, while I wandered where the huddling rill
Brightens with water-breaks the hollow ghyll
As by enchantment, an obscure retreat
Opened at once, and stayed my devious feet.
While thick above the rill the branches close,
In rocky basin its wild waves repose,
Inverted shrubs, and moss of gloomy green,
Cling from the rocks, with pale wood-weeds
        between;
And its own twilight softens the whole scene,
Save where aloft the subtle sunbeams shine
On withered briars that o'er the crags recline;
Save where, with sparkling foam, a small cascade
Illumines, from within, the leafy shade;
Beyond, along the vista of the brook,
Where antique roots its bustling course o'erlook,
The eye reposes on a secret bridge
Half grey, half shagged with ivy to its ridge;
There, bending o'er the stream, the listless swain
Lingers behind his disappearing wain.

    – Did Sabine grace adorn my living line,
Blandusia's praise, wild stream, should yield to
        thine!
Never shall ruthless minister of death
'Mid thy soft glooms the glittering steel unsheath;
No goblets shall, for thee, be crowned with flowers,
No kid with piteous outcry thrill thy bowers;

The mystic shapes that by thy margin rove
A more benignant sacrifice approve –
A mind, that, in a calm angelic mood
Of happy wisdom, meditating good,
Beholds, of all from her high powers required,
Much done, and much designed, and more desired, –
Harmonious thoughts, a soul by truth refined,
Entire affection for all human kind.

  Dear Brook, farewell! To-morrow's noon again
Shall hide me, wooing long thy wildwood strain;
But now the sun has gained his western road,
And eve's mild hour invites my steps abroad.
While, near the midway cliff, the silvered kite
In many a whistling circle wheels her flight;
Slant watery lights, from parting clouds, apace
Travel along the precipice's base;
Cheering its naked waste of scattered stone,
By lichens grey, and scanty moss, o'ergrown;
Where scarce the foxglove peeps, or thistle's beard;
And restless stone-chat, all day long, is heard.

  How pleasant, as the sun declines, to view
The spacious landscape change in form and hue!
Here, vanish, as in mist, before a flood
Of bright obscurity, hill, lawn, and wood;
There, objects, by the searching beams betrayed,
Come forth, and here retire in purple shade;
Even the white stems of birch, the cottage white,
Soften their glare before the mellow light;
The skiffs, at anchor where with umbrage wide

Yon chestnuts half the latticed boat-house hide,
Shed from their sides, that face the sun's slant
 beam,
Strong flakes of radiance on the tremulous stream:
Raised by yon travelling flock, a dusty cloud
Mounts from the road, and spreads its moving
 shroud;
The shepherd, all involved in wreaths of fire,
Now shows a shadowy speck, and now is lost
 entire.

Into a gradual calm the breezes sink,
A blue rim borders all the lake's still brink;
There doth the twinkling aspen's foliage sleep,
And insects clothe, like dust, the glassy deep:
And now, on every side, the surface breaks
Into blue spots, and slowly lengthening streaks;
Here, plots of sparkling water tremble bright
With thousand thousand twinkling points of light;
There, waves that, hardly weltering, die away,
Tip their smooth ridges with a softer ray;
And now the whole wide lake in deep repose
Is hushed, and like a burnished mirror glows,
Save where, along the shady western marge,
Coasts, with industrious oar, the charcoal barge.

Their panniered train a group of potters goad,
Winding from side to side up the steep road;
The peasant, from yon cliff of fearful edge
Shot, down the headlong path darts with his
 sledge;

Bright beams the lonely mountain-horse illume
Feeding 'mid purple heath, 'green rings', and
    broom;
While the sharp slope the slackened team
    confounds,
Downward the ponderous timber-wain resounds;
In foamy breaks the rill, with merry song,
Dashed o'er the rough rock, lightly leaps along;
From lonesome chapel at the mountain's feet,
Three humble bells their rustic chime repeat;
Sounds from the water-side the hammered boat;
And blasted' quarry thunders, heard remote!

  Even here, amid the sweep of endless woods,
Blue pomp of lakes, high cliffs, and falling floods,
Not undelightful are the simplest charms,
Found by the grassy door of mountain-farms.

   Sweetly ferocious, round his native walks,
Pride of his sister-wives, the monarch stalks;
Spur-clad his nervous feet, and firm his tread;
A crest of purple tops the warrior's head.
Bright sparks his black and rolling eye-ball hurls
Afar, his tail he closes and unfurls;
On tiptoe reared, he strains his clarion throat,
Threatened by faintly-answering farms remote:
Again with his shrill voice the mountain rings,
While, flapped with conscious pride, resound his
    wings.

  Where, mixed with graceful birch, the sombrous
    pine

And yew-tree o'er the silver rocks recline;
I love to mark the quarry's moving trains,
Dwarf panniered steeds, and men, and numerous
     wains;
How busy all the enormous hive within,
While Echo dallies with its various din!
Some (hear yon not their chisels' clinking sound?)
Toil, small as pigmies in the gulf profound;
Some, dim between the lofty cliffs descried,
O'erwalk the slender plank from side to side;
These, by the pale-blue rocks that ceaseless ring,
In airy baskets hanging, work and sing.

   Just where a cloud above the mountain rears
An edge all flame, the broadening sun appears;
A long blue bar its aegis orb divides,
And breaks the spreading of its golden tides;
And now that orb has touched the purple steep
Whose softened image penetrates the deep.

   'Cross the calm lake's blue shades the cliffs aspire,
With towers and woods, a 'prospect all on fire',
While coves and secret hollows, through a ray
Of fainter gold, a purple gleam betray.
Each slip of lawn the broken rocks between
Shines in the light with more than earthly green:
Deep yellow beams the scattered stems illume,
Far in the level forest's central gloom:
Waving his hat, the shepherd, from the vale,
Directs his winding dog the cliffs to scale, –
The dog, loud barking, 'mid the glittering rocks,

Hunts, where his master points, the intercepted
    flocks.
Where oaks o'erhang the road the radiance shoots
On tawny earth, wild weeds, and twisted roots;
The druid-stones a brightened ring unfold;
And all the babbling brooks are liquid gold;
Sunk to a curve, the day-star lessens still,
Gives one bright glance, and drops behind the hill.
    In these secluded vales, if village fame,
Confirmed by hoary hairs, belief may claim;
When up the hills, as now, retired the light,
Strange apparitions mocked the shepherd's sight.
    The form appears of one that spurs his steed
Midway along the hill with desperate speed;
Unhurt pursues his lengthened flight, while all
Attend, at every stretch, his headlong fall.
Anon, appears a brave, a gorgeous show
Of horsemen-shadows moving to and fro;
At intervals imperial banners stream,
And now the van reflects the solar beam;
The rear through iron brown betrays a sullen
    gleam.
While silent stands the admiring crowd below,
Silent the visionary warriors go,
Winding in ordered pomp their upward way
Till the last banner of the long array
Has disappeared, and every trace is fled
Of splendour – save the beacon's spiry head
Tipt with eve's latest gleam of burning red.

Now, while the solemn evening shadows sail,
On slowly-waving pinions, down the vale;
And, fronting the bright west, yon oak entwines
Its darkening boughs and leaves, in stronger lines;
'Tis pleasant near the tranquil lake to stray
Where, winding on along some secret bay,
The swan uplifts his chest, and backward flings
His neck, a varying arch, between his towering
    wings:
The eye that marks the gliding creature sees
How graceful, pride can be, and how majestic, ease,
    While tender cares and mild domestic loves
With furtive watch pursue her as she moves,
The female with a meeker charm succeeds,
And her brown little-ones around her leads,
Nibbling the water lilies as they pass,
Or playing wanton with the floating grass.
She, in a mother's care, her beauty's pride
Forgetting, calls the wearied to her side;
Alternately they mount her back, and rest
Close by her mantling wings' embraces prest.
    Long may they float upon this flood serene;
Theirs be these holms untrodden, still, and green,
Where leafy shades fence off the blustering gale,
And breathes in peace the lily of the vale!
Yon isle, which feels not even the milkmaid's feet,
Yet hears her song, 'by distance made more sweet',
Yon isle conceals their home, their hut-like bower;
Green water-rushes overspread the floor;

10

Long grass and willows form the woven wall,
And swings above the roof the poplar tall.
Thence issuing often with unwieldy stalk,
They crush with broad black feet their flowery walk;
Or, from the neighbouring water, hear at morn
The hound, the horse's tread, and mellow horn;
Involve their serpent-necks in changeful rings,
Rolled wantonly between their slippery wings,
Or, starting up with noise and rude delight,
Force half upon the wave their cumbrous flight.

Fair Swan! by all a mother's joys caressed,
Haply some wretch has eyed, and called thee
   blessed;
When with her infants, from some shady seat
By the lake's edge, she rose – to face the noontide
   heat;
Or taught their limbs along the dusty road
A few short steps to totter with their load.

I see her now, denied to lay her head,
On cold blue nights, in hut or straw-built shed,
Turn to a silent smile their sleepy cry,
By pointing to the gliding moon on high.
– When low-hung clouds each star of summer hide,
And fireless are the valleys far and wide,
Where the brook brawls along the public road
Dark with bat-haunted ashes stretching broad,
Oft has she taught them on her lap to lay
The shining glow-worm; or, in heedless play,
Toss it from hand to hand, disquieted;

While others, not unseen, are free to shed
Green unmolested light upon their mossy bed.
    Oh! when the sleety showers her path assail,
And like a torrent roars the headstrong gale;
No more her breath can thaw their fingers cold,
Their frozen arms her neck no more can fold;
Weak roof a cowering form two babes to shield,
And faint the fire a dying heart can yield!
Press the sad kiss, fond mother! vainly fears
Thy flooded cheek to wet them with its tears;
No tears can chill them, and no bosom warms,
Thy breast their death-bed, coffined in thine arms!
    Sweet are the sounds that mingle from afar,
Heard by calm lakes, as peeps the folding star,
Where the duck dabbles 'mid the rustling sedge,
And feeding pike starts from the water's edge,
Or the swan stirs the reeds, his neck and bill
Wetting, that drip upon the water still;
And heron, as resounds the trodden shore,
Shoots upward, darting his long neck before.
    Now, with religious awe, the farewell light
Blends with the solemn colouring of night;
'Mid groves of clouds that crest the mountain's
        brow,
And round the west's proud lodge their shadows
        throw,
Like Una shining on her gloomy way,
The half-seen form of Twilight roams astray;
Shedding, through paly loop-holes mild and small,

Gleams that upon the lake's still bosom fall;
Soft o'er the surface creep those lustres pale
Tracking the motions of the fitful gale.
With restless interchange at once the bright
Wins on the shade, the shade upon the light.
No favoured eye was e'er allowed to gaze
On lovelier spectacle in faery days;
When gentle Spirits urged a sportive chase,
Brushing with lucid wands the water's face:
While music, stealing round the glimmering deeps,
Charmed the tall circle of the enchanted steeps.
– The lights are vanished from the watery plains:
No wreck of all the pageantry remains.
Unheeded night has overcome the vales:
On the dark earth the wearied vision fails;
The latest lingerer of the forest train,
The lone black fir, forsakes the faded plain;
Last evening sight, the cottage smoke, no more,
Lost in the thickened darkness, glimmers hoar;
And, towering from the sullen dark-brown mere,
Like a black wall, the mountain-steeps appear.
– Now o'er the soothed accordant heart we feel
A sympathetic twilight slowly steal,
And ever, as we fondly muse, we find
The soft gloom deepening on the tranquil mind.
Stay! pensive, sadly-pleasing visions, stay!
Ah no! as fades the vale, they fade away:
Yet still the tender, vacant gloom remains;
Still the cold cheek its shuddering tear retains.

The bird, who ceased, with fading light, to thread
Silent the hedge or steamy rivulet's bed,
From his grey re-appearing tower shall soon
Salute with gladsome note the rising moon,
While with a hoary light she frosts the ground,
And pours a deeper blue to Aether's bound;
Pleased, as she moves, her pomp of clouds to fold
In robes of azure, fleecy-white, and gold.

Above yon eastern hill, where darkness broods
O'er all its vanished dells, and lawns, and woods;
Where but a mass of shade the sight can trace,
Even now she shews, half-veiled, her lovely face:
Across the gloomy valley flings her light,
Far to the western slopes with hamlets white;
And gives, where woods the chequered upland
    strew,
To the green corn of summer, autumn's hue.

Thus Hope, first pouring from her blessed horn
Her dawn, far lovelier than the moon's own morn,
Till higher mounted, strives in vain to cheer
The weary hills, impervious, blackening near;
Yet does she still, undaunted, throw the while
On darling spots remote her tempting smile.

Even now she decks for me a distant scene,
(For dark and broad the gulf of time between)
Gilding that cottage with her fondest ray,
(Sole bourn, sole wish, sole object of my way;
How fair its lawns and sheltering woods appear!
How sweet its streamlet murmurs in mine ear!)

Where we, my Friend, to happy days shall rise,
Till our small share of hardly-paining sighs
(For sighs will ever trouble human breath)
Creep hushed into the tranquil breast of death.

But now the clear bright Moon her zenith gains,
And, rimy without speck, extend the plains:
The deepest cleft the mountain's front displays
Scarce hides a shadow from her searching rays;
From the dark-blue faint silvery threads divide
The hills, while gleams below the azure tide;
Time softly treads; throughout the landscape
    breathes
A peace enlivened, not disturbed, by wreaths
Of charcoal-smoke, that o'er the fallen wood,
Steal down the hill, and spread along the flood.

The song of mountain-streams, unheard by day,
Now hardly heard, beguiles my homeward way.
Air listens, like the sleeping water, still,
To catch the spiritual music of the hill,
Broke only by the slow clock tolling deep,
Or shout that wakes the ferry-man from sleep,
The echoed hoof nearing the distant shore,
The boat's first motion – made with dashing oar;
Sound of closed gate, across the water borne,
Hurrying the timid hare through rustling corn;
The sportive outcry of the mocking owl;
And at long intervals the mill-dog's howl;
The distant forge's swinging thump profound;
Or yell, in the deep woods, of lonely hound.

– Lines Written in Early Spring (1798) –

I heard a thousand blended notes,
While in a grove I sate reclined,
In that sweet mood when pleasant thoughts
Bring sad thoughts to the mind.

To her fair works did Nature link
The human soul that through me ran;
And much it grieved my heart to think
What man has made of man.

Through primrose tufts, in that green bower,
The periwinkle trailed its wreaths;
And 'tis my faith that every flower
Enjoys the air it breathes.

The birds around me hopped and played,
Their thoughts I cannot measure: –
But the least motion which they made
It seemed a thrill of pleasure.

The budding twigs spread out their fan,
To catch the breezy air;
And I must think, do all I can,
That there was pleasure there.

If this belief from heaven be sent,
If such be Nature's holy plan,
Have I not reason to lament
What man has made of man?

– Tintern Abbey (1798) –

Five years have past; five summers, with the length
Of five long winters! and again I hear
These waters, rolling from their mountain-springs
With a soft inland murmur. – Once again
Do I behold these steep and lofty cliffs,
That on a wild secluded scene impress
Thoughts of more deep seclusion; and connect
The landscape with the quiet of the sky.
The day is come when I again repose
Here, under this dark sycamore, and view
These plots of cottage-ground, these orchard-tufts,
Which at this season, with their unripe fruits,
Are clad in one green hue, and lose themselves
'Mid groves and copses. Once again I see
These hedge-rows, hardly hedge-rows, little lines
Of sportive wood run wild: these pastoral farms,
Green to the very door; and wreaths of smoke
Sent up, in silence, from among the trees!
With some uncertain notice, as might seem
Of vagrant dwellers in the houseless woods,
Or of some Hermit's cave, where by his fire
The Hermit sits alone.
                            These beauteous forms,
Through a long absence, have not been to me
As is a landscape to a blind man's eye:
But oft, in lonely rooms, and 'mid the din
Of towns and cities, I have owed to them,

In hours of weariness, sensations sweet,
Felt in the blood, and felt along the heart;
And passing even into my purer mind,
With tranquil restoration: – feelings too
Of unremembered pleasure: such, perhaps,
As have no slight or trivial influence
On that best portion of a good man's life,
His little, nameless, unremembered, acts
Of kindness and of love. Nor less, I trust,
To them I may have owed another gift,
Of aspect more sublime; that blessed mood,
In which the burthen of the mystery,
In which the heavy and the weary weight
Of all this unintelligible world,
Is lightened: – that serene and blessed mood,
In which the affections gently lead us on, –
Until, the breath of this corporeal frame
And even the motion of our human blood
Almost suspended, we are laid asleep
In body, and become a living soul:
While with an eye made quiet by the power
Of harmony, and the deep power of joy,
We see into the life of things.
                            If this
Be but a vain belief, yet, oh! how oft –
In darkness and amid the many shapes
Of joyless daylight; when the fretful stir
Unprofitable, and the fever of the world,
Have hung upon the beatings of my heart –

How oft, in spirit, have I turned to thee,
O sylvan Wye! thou wanderer thro' the woods,
How often has my spirit turned to thee!
   And now, with gleams of half-extinguished thought,
With many recognitions dim and faint,
And somewhat of a sad perplexity,
The picture of the mind revives again:
While here I stand, not only with the sense
Of present pleasure, but with pleasing thoughts
That in this moment there is life and food
For future years. And so I dare to hope,
Though changed, no doubt, from what I was when
     first
I came among these hills; when like a roe
I bounded o'er the mountains, by the sides
Of the deep rivers, and the lonely streams,
Wherever nature led: more like a man
Flying from something that he dreads than one
Who sought the thing he loved. For nature then
(The coarser pleasures of my boyish days,
And their glad animal movements all gone by)
To me was all in all. – I cannot paint
What then I was. The sounding cataract
Haunted me like a passion: the tall rock,
The mountain, and the deep and gloomy wood,
Their colours and their forms, were then to me
An appetite; a feeling and a love,
That had no need of a remoter charm,
By thought supplied, nor any interest

Unborrowed from the eye. – That time is past,
And all its aching joys are now no more,
And all its dizzy raptures. Not for this
Faint I, nor mourn nor murmur; other gifts
Have followed; for such loss, I would believe,
Abundant recompense. For I have learned
To look on nature, not as in the hour
Of thoughtless youth; but hearing often-times
The still, sad music of humanity,
Nor harsh nor grating, though of ample power
To chasten and subdue. – And I have felt
A presence that disturbs me with the joy
Of elevated thoughts; a sense sublime
Of something far more deeply interfused,
Whose dwelling is the light of setting suns,
And the round ocean and the living air,
And the blue sky, and in the mind of man:
A motion and a spirit, that impels
All thinking things, all objects of all thought,
And rolls through all things. Therefore am I still
A lover of the meadows and the woods,
And mountains; and of all that we behold
From this green earth; of all the mighty world
Of eye, and ear, – both what they half create,
And what perceive; well pleased to recognise
In nature and the language of the sense
The anchor of my purest thoughts, the nurse,
The guide, the guardian of my heart, and soul
Of all my moral being.

                    Nor perchance,
If I were not thus taught, should I the more
Suffer my genial spirits to decay:
For thou art with me here upon the banks
Of this fair river; thou my dearest Friend,
My dear, dear Friend; and in thy voice I catch
The language of my former heart, and read
My former pleasures in the shooting lights
Of thy wild eyes. Oh! yet a little while
May I behold in thee what I was once,
My dear, dear Sister! and this prayer I make,
Knowing that Nature never did betray
The heart that loved her; 'tis her privilege,
Through all the years of this our life, to lead
From joy to joy: for she can so inform
The mind that is within us, so impress
With quietness and beauty, and so feed
With lofty thoughts, that neither evil tongues,
Rash judgments, nor the sneers of selfish men,
Nor greetings where no kindness is, nor all
The dreary intercourse of daily life,
Shall e'er prevail against us, or disturb
Our cheerful faith, that all which we behold
Is full of blessings. Therefore let the moon
Shine on thee in thy solitary walk;
And let the misty mountain-winds be free
To blow against thee: and, in after years,
When these wild ecstasies shall be matured
Into a sober pleasure; when thy mind

Shall be a mansion for all lovely forms,
Thy memory be as a dwelling-place
For all sweet sounds and harmonies; oh! then,
If solitude, or fear, or pain, or grief,
Should be thy portion, with what healing thoughts
Of tender joy wilt thou remember me,
And these my exhortations! Nor, perchance –
If I should be where I no more can hear
Thy voice, nor catch from thy wild eyes these
        gleams
Of past existence – wilt thou, then forget
That on the banks of this delightful stream
We stood together; and that I, so long
A worshipper of Nature, hither came
Unwearied in that service: rather say
With warmer love – oh! with far deeper zeal
Of holier love. Nor wilt thou then forget
That after many wanderings, many years
Of absence, these steep woods and lofty cliffs,
And this green pastoral landscape, were to me
More dear, both for themselves and for thy sake!

– The Old Cumberland Beggar (1798) –

I saw an aged Beggar in my walk;
And he was seated, by the highway side,
On a low structure of rude masonry
Built at the foot of a huge hill, that they
Who lead their horses down the steep rough road
May thence remount at ease. The aged Man
Had placed his staff across the broad smooth stone
That overlays the pile; and, from a bag
All white with flour, the dole of village dames,
He drew his scraps and fragments, one by one;
And scanned them with a fixed and serious look
Of idle computation. In the sun,
Upon the second step of that small pile,
Surrounded by those wild, unpeopled hills,
He sat, and ate his food in solitude:
And ever, scattered from his palsied hand,
That, still attempting to prevent the waste,
Was baffled still, the crumbs in little showers
Fell on the ground; and the small mountain birds
Not venturing yet to peck their destined meal,
Approached within the length of half his staff.
Him from my childhood have I known; and then
He was so old, he seems not older now;
He travels on, a solitary Man,
So helpless in appearance, that from him
The sauntering Horseman throws not with a slack
And careless hand his alms upon the ground,

But stops, – that he may safely lodge the coin
Within the old Man's hat; nor quits him so,
But still, when he has given his horse the rein,
Watches the aged Beggar with a look
Sidelong, and half-reverted. She who tends
The toll-gate, when in summer at her door
She turns her wheel, if on the road she sees
The aged Beggar coming, quits her work,
And lifts the latch for him that he may pass.
The post-boy, when his rattling wheels o'ertake
The aged Beggar in the woody lane,
Shouts to him from behind; and if, thus warned,
The old Man does not change his course, the boy
Turns with less noisy wheels to the roadside,
And passes gently by, without a curse
Upon his lips, or anger at his heart.
He travels on, a solitary Man;
His age has no companion. On the ground
His eyes are turned, and, as he moves along,
They move along the ground; and, evermore,
Instead of common and habitual sight
Of fields, with rural works, of hill and dale,
And the blue sky, one little span of earth
Is all his prospect. Thus, from day to day,
Bow-bent, his eyes forever on the ground,
He plies his weary journey; seeing still,
And seldom knowing that he sees, some straw,
Some scattered leaf, or marks which, in one track,
The nails of cart or chariot-wheel have left

Impressed on the white road, – in the same line,
At distance still the same. Poor Traveller!
His staff trails with him; scarcely do his feet
Disturb the summer dust; he is so still
In look and motion, that the cottage curs,
Ere he has passed the door, will turn away,
Weary of barking at him. Boys and girls,
The vacant and the busy, maids and youths,
And urchins newly breeched – all pass him by:
Him even the slow-paced waggon leaves behind.
But deem not this Man useless. – Statesmen! ye
Who are so restless in your wisdom, ye
Who have a broom still ready in your hands
To rid the world of nuisances; ye proud,
Heart-swoln, while in your pride ye contemplate
Your talents, power, or wisdom, deem him not
A burden of the earth! 'Tis Nature's law
That none, the meanest of created things,
Of forms created the most vile and brute,
The dullest or most noxious, should exist
Divorced from good – a spirit and pulse of good,
A life and soul, to every mode of being
Inseparably linked. Then be assured
That least of all can aught – that ever owned
The heaven-regarding eye and front sublime
Which man is born to – sink, howe'er depressed,
So low as to be scorned without a sin;
Without offence to God cast out of view;
Like the dry remnant of a garden-flower

Whose seeds are shed, or as an implement
Worn out and worthless. While from door to door,
This old Man creeps, the villagers in him
Behold a record which together binds
Past deeds and offices of charity,
Else unremembered, and so keeps alive
The kindly mood in hearts which lapse of years,
And that half-wisdom half-experience gives,
Make slow to feel, and by sure steps resign
To selfishness and cold oblivious cares,
Among the farms and solitary huts,
Hamlets and thinly-scattered villages,
Where'er the aged Beggar takes his rounds,
The mild necessity of use compels
The acts of love; and habit does the work
Of reason; yet prepares that after-joy
Which reason cherishes. And thus the soul,
By that sweet taste of pleasure unpursued,
Doth find herself insensibly disposed
To virtue and true goodness.

                    Some there are
By their good works exalted, lofty minds
And meditative, authors of delight
And happiness, which to the end of time
Will live, and spread, and kindle: even such minds
In childhood, from this solitary Being,
Or from like wanderer, haply have received
(A thing more precious far than all that books

Or the solicitudes of love can do!)
That first mild touch of sympathy and thought,
In which they found their kindred with a world
Where want and sorrow were. The easy man
Who sits at his own door, – and, like the pear
That overhangs his head from the green wall,
Feeds in the sunshine; the robust and young,
The prosperous and unthinking, they who live
Sheltered, and flourish in a little grove
Of their own kindred; – all behold in him
A silent monitor, which on their minds
Must needs impress a transitory thought
Of self-congratulation, to the heart
Of each recalling his peculiar boons,
His charters and exemptions; and, perchance,
Though he to no one give the fortitude
And circumspection needful to preserve
His present blessings, and to husband up
The respite of the season, he, at least,
And 't is no vulgar service, makes them felt.

Yet further. – Many, I believe, there are
Who live a life of virtuous decency,
Men who can hear the Decalogue and feel
No self-reproach; who of the moral law
Established in the land where they abide
Are strict observers; and not negligent
In acts of love to those with whom they dwell,
Their kindred, and the children of their blood.

Praise be to such, and to their slumbers peace!
But of the poor man ask, the abject poor;
Go, and demand of him, if there be here
In this cold abstinence from evil deeds,
And these inevitable charities,
Wherewith to satisfy the human soul?
No – man is dear to man; the poorest poor
Long for some moments in a weary life
When they can know and feel that they have been,
Themselves, the fathers and the dealers-out
Of some small blessings; have been kind to such
As needed kindness, for this single cause,
That we have all of us one human heart.
 – Such pleasure is to one kind Being known,
My neighbour, when with punctual care, each week
Duly as Friday comes, though pressed herself
By her own wants, she from her store of meal
Takes one unsparing handful for the scrip
Of this old Mendicant, and, from her door
Returning with exhilarated heart,
Sits by her fire, and builds her hope in heaven.

Then let him pass, a blessing on his head!
And while in that vast solitude to which
The tide of things has borne him, he appears
To breathe and live but for himself alone,
Unblamed, uninjured, let him bear about
The good which the benignant law of Heaven
Has hung around him: and, while life is his,

Still let him prompt the unlettered villagers
To tender offices and pensive thoughts.
 – Then let him pass, a blessing on his head!
And, long as he can wander, let him breathe
The freshness of the valleys; let his blood
Struggle with frosty air and winter snows;
And let the chartered wind that sweeps the heath
Beat his grey locks against his withered face.
Reverence the hope whose vital anxiousness
Gives the last human interest to his heart.
May never HOUSE, misnamed of INDUSTRY,
Make him a captive! – for that pent-up din,
Those life-consuming sounds that clog the air,
Be his the natural silence of old age!
Let him be free of mountain solitudes;
And have around him, whether heard or not,
The pleasant melody of woodland birds.
Few are his pleasures: if his eyes have now
Been doomed so long to settle upon earth
That not without some effort they behold
The countenance of the horizontal sun,
Rising or setting, let the light at least
Find a free entrance to their languid orbs.
And let him, where and when he will, sit down
Beneath the trees, or on a grassy bank
Of highway side, and with the little birds
Share his chance-gathered meal; and, finally,
As in the eye of Nature he has lived,
So in the eye of Nature let him die!

– To My Sister (1798) –

It is the first mild day of March:
Each minute sweeter than before
The redbreast sings from the tall larch
That stands beside our door.

There is a blessing in the air,
Which seems a sense of joy to yield
To the bare trees, and mountains bare,
And grass in the green field.

My sister! ('tis a wish of mine)
Now that our morning meal is done,
Make haste, your morning task resign;
Come forth and feel the sun.

Edward will come with you; – and, pray,
Put on with speed your woodland dress;
And bring no book: for this one day
We'll give to idleness.

No joyless forms shall regulate
Our living calendar:
We from to-day, my Friend, will date
The opening of the year.

Love, now a universal birth,
From heart to heart is stealing,
From earth to man, from man to earth:
– It is the hour of feeling.

One moment now may give us more
Than years of toiling reason:
Our minds shall drink at every pore
The spirit of the season.

Some silent laws our hearts will make,
Which they shall long obey:
We for the year to come may take
Our temper from to-day.

And from the blessed power that rolls
About, below, above,
We'll frame the measure of our souls:
They shall be tuned to love.

Then come, my Sister! come, I pray,
With speed put on your woodland dress;
And bring no book: for this one day
We'll give to idleness.

– There Was a Boy (1798) –

There was a boy: ye knew him well, ye cliffs
And islands of Winander! – many a time
At evening, when the earliest stars began
To move along the edges of the hills,
Rising or setting, would he stand alone
Beneath the trees or by the glimmering lake,
And there, with fingers interwoven, both hands
Pressed closely palm to palm, and to his mouth
Uplifted, he, as through an instrument,
Blew mimic hootings to the silent owls,
That they might answer him; and they would shout
Across the watery vale, and shout again,
Responsive to his call, with quivering peals,
And long halloos and screams, and echoes loud,
Redoubled and redoubled, concourse wild
Of jocund din; and, when a lengthened pause
Of silence came and baffled his best skill,
Then sometimes, in that silence while he hung
Listening, a gentle shock of mild surprise
Has carried far into his heart the voice
Of mountain-torrents; or the visible scene
Would enter unawares into his mind,
With all its solemn imagery, its rocks,
Its woods, and that uncertain heaven, received
Into the bosom of the steady lake.

This boy was taken from his mates, and died
In childhood, ere he was full twelve years old.
Pre-eminent in beauty is the vale
Where he was born and bred: the churchyard hangs
Upon a slope above the village-school;
And through that churchyard when my way has led
On summer-evenings, I believe that there
A long half-hour together I have stood
Mute – looking at the grave in which he lies!

– *from* Preface to the Second Edition of the *Lyrical Ballads* (1800) –

It is supposed, that by the act of writing in verse an Author makes a formal engagement that he will gratify certain known habits of association; that he not only thus apprises the Reader that certain classes of ideas and expressions will be found in his book, but that others will be carefully excluded. This exponent or symbol held forth by metrical language must in different eras of literature have excited very different expectations: for example, in the age of Catullus, Terence, and Lucretius, and that of Statius or Claudian; and in our own country, in the age of Shakespeare and Beaumont and Fletcher, and that of Donne and Cowley, or Dryden, or Pope. I will not take upon me to determine the exact import of the promise which, by the act of writing in verse, an Author in the present day makes to his reader: but it will undoubtedly appear to many persons that I have not fulfilled the terms of an engagement thus voluntarily contracted. They who have been accustomed to the gaudiness and inane phraseology of many modern writers, if they persist in reading this book to its conclusion, will, no doubt, frequently have to struggle with feelings of strangeness and awkwardness: they will look round for poetry, and will be induced to inquire by what species of courtesy these attempts can be permitted to assume that title. I hope therefore the reader will not censure me for attempting to state what I have proposed to myself to perform; and also (as far as the limits of a preface will permit) to explain some of the chief reasons which have determined me in the choice of my purpose: that at least he may be spared any unpleasant feeling of disappointment, and that I myself may be protected from one of the most dishonourable accusations which can be brought against an Author, namely, that of an indolence which prevents him from endeavouring to ascertain what is his duty, or, when his duty is ascertained, prevents him from performing it.

The principal object, then, proposed in these Poems was to choose incidents and situations from common life, and to relate or describe them, throughout, as far as was possible in a selection of language really used by men, and, at the same time, to throw over them a certain colouring of imagination, whereby ordinary things should be presented to the mind in an unusual aspect; and, further, and above all, to make these incidents and situations interesting by tracing in them, truly though not ostentatiously, the primary laws of our nature: chiefly, as far as regards the manner in which we associate ideas in a state of excitement. Humble and rustic life was generally chosen, because, in that condition, the essential passions of the heart find a better soil in which they can attain their maturity, are less under restraint, and speak a plainer and more emphatic language; because in that condition of life our elementary feelings coexist in a state of greater simplicity, and, consequently, may be more accurately contemplated, and more forcibly communicated; because the manners of rural life germinate from those elementary feelings, and, from the necessary character of rural occupations, are more easily comprehended, and are more durable; and, lastly, because in that condition the passions of men are incorporated with the beautiful and permanent forms of nature. The language, too, of these men has been adopted (purified indeed from what appear to be its real defects, from all lasting and rational causes of dislike or disgust) because such men hourly communicate with the best objects from which the best part of language is originally derived; and because, from their rank in society and the sameness and narrow circle of their intercourse, being less under the influence of social vanity, they convey their feelings and notions in simple and unelaborated expressions. Accordingly, such a language, arising out of repeated experience and regular feelings, is a more permanent, and a far more philosophical language, than that which is frequently substituted for it by Poets, who think that they are conferring honour upon themselves and their art, in proportion as they separate themselves from the sympathies of men, and indulge in arbitrary and capricious habits of expression, in order to furnish food for fickle tastes, and fickle appetites, of their own creation.

– A Narrow Girdle of Rough Stones and Crags (1800) –

A narrow girdle of rough stones and crags,
A rude and natural causeway, interposed
Between the water and a winding slope
Of copse and thicket, leaves the eastern shore
Of Grasmere safe in its own privacy:
And there myself and two beloved Friends,
One calm September morning, ere the mist
Had altogether yielded to the sun,

Sauntered on this retired and difficult way.
– Ill suits the road with one in haste; but we
Played with our time; and, as we strolled along,
It was our occupation to observe
Such objects as the waves had tossed ashore –
Feather, or leaf, or weed, or withered bough,
Each on the other heaped, along the line
Of the dry wreck. And, in our vacant mood,
Not seldom did we stop to watch some tuft
Of dandelion seed or thistle's beard,
That skimmed the surface of the dead calm lake,
Suddenly halting now – a lifeless stand!
And starting off again with freak as sudden;
In all its sportive wanderings, all the while,
Making report of an invisible breeze
That was its wings, its chariot, and its horse,
Its playmate, rather say, its moving soul.
– And often, trifling with a privilege
Alike indulged to all, we paused, one now,
And now the other, to point out, perchance
To pluck, some flower or water-weed, too fair
Either to be divided from the place
On which it grew, or to be left alone
To its own beauty. Many such there are,
Fair ferns and flowers, and chiefly that tall fern,
So stately, of the queen Osmunda named;
Plant lovelier, in its own retired abode
On Grasmere's beach, than Naiad by the side
Of Grecian brook, or Lady of the Mere,

Sole-sitting by the shores of old romance.
– So fared we that bright morning: from the fields
Meanwhile, a noise was heard, the busy mirth
Of reapers, men and women, boys and girls.
Delighted much to listen to those sounds,
And feeding thus our fancies, we advanced
Along the indented shore; when suddenly,
Through a thin veil of glittering haze was seen
Before us, on a point of jutting land,
The tall and upright figure of a Man
Attired in peasant's garb, who stood alone,
Angling beside the margin of the lake.
'Improvident and reckless,' we exclaimed,
'The Man must be, who thus can lose a day
Of the mid harvest, when the labourer's hire
Is ample, and some little might be stored
Wherewith to cheer him in the winter time.'
Thus talking of that Peasant, we approached
Close to the spot where with his rod and line
He stood alone; whereat he turned his head
To greet us – and we saw a Mam worn down
By sickness, gaunt and lean, with sunken cheeks
And wasted limbs, his legs so long and lean
That for my single self I looked at them,
Forgetful of the body they sustained. –
Too weak to labour in the harvest field,
The Man was using his best skill to gain
A pittance from the dead unfeeling lake
That knew not of his wants. I will not say

What thoughts immediately were ours, nor how
The happy idleness of that sweet morn,
With all its lovely images, was changed
To serious musing and to self-reproach.
Nor did we fail to see within ourselves
What need there is to be reserved in speech,
And temper all our thoughts with charity.
– Therefore, unwilling to forget that day,
My Friend, Myself, and She who then received
The same admonishment, have called the place
By a memorial name, uncouth indeed
As e'er by mariner was given to bay
Or foreland, on a new-discovered coast;
And POINT RASH-JUDGMENT is the name it bears.

– I Wander'd Lonely as a Cloud (1804) –
(also known as 'Daffodils')

I wander'd lonely as a cloud
That floats on high o'er vales and hills,
When all at once I saw a crowd,
A host of golden daffodils,
Beside the lake, beneath the trees
Fluttering and dancing in the breeze.
Continuous as the stars that shine
And twinkle on the milky way,
They stretch'd in never-ending line

Along the margin of a bay:
Ten thousand saw I at a glance
Tossing their heads in sprightly dance.
The waves beside them danced, but they
Out-did the sparkling waves in glee:
A poet could not but be gay
In such a jocund company!
I gazed – and gazed – but little thought
What wealth the show to me had brought.
For oft, when on my couch I lie
In vacant or in pensive mood,
They flash upon that inward eye
Which is the bliss of solitude;
And then my heart with pleasure fills
And dances with the daffodils.

– Ode: Intimations of Immortality from
Recollections of Early Childhood (1804) –

I

There was a time when meadow, grove, and stream,
The earth, and every common sight
To me did seem
Apparelled in celestial light,
The glory and the freshness of a dream.
It is not now as it hath been of yore;–

Turn wheresoe'er I may,
By night or day,
The things which I have seen I now can see no more.

II

The rainbow comes and goes,
And lovely is the rose;
The moon doth with delight
Look round her when the heavens are bare;
Waters on a starry night
Are beautiful and fair;
The sunshine is a glorious birth;
But yet I know, where'er I go,
That there hath past away a glory from the earth.

III

Now, while the birds thus sing a joyous song,
And while the young lambs bound
As to the tabor's sound,
To me alone there came a thought of grief:
A timely utterance gave that thought relief,
And I again am strong.
The cataracts blow their trumpets from the steep,
No more shall grief of mine the season wrong:
I hear the echoes through the mountains throng.
The winds come to me from the fields of sleep,
And all the earth is gay;

Land and sea
Give themselves up to jollity,
And with the heart of May
Doth every beast keep holiday;–
Thou child of joy,
Shout round me, let me hear thy shouts, thou happy
Shepherd-boy!

IV

Ye blessèd Creatures, I have heard the call
Ye to each other make; I see
The heavens laugh with you in your jubilee;
My heart is at your festival,
My head hath its coronal,
The fulness of your bliss, I feel – I feel it all.
O evil day! if I were sullen
While Earth herself is adorning
This sweet May-morning;
And the children are culling
On every side
In a thousand valleys far and wide
Fresh flowers; while the sun shines warm,
And the babe leaps up on his mother's arm:–
I hear, I hear, with joy I hear!
– But there's a tree, of many, one,
A single field which I have look'd upon,
Both of them speak of something that is gone:

The pansy at my feet
Doth the same tale repeat:
Whither is fled the visionary gleam?
Where is it now, the glory and the dream?

V

Our birth is but a sleep and a forgetting;
The Soul that rises with us, our life's Star,
Hath had elsewhere its setting
And cometh from afar;
Not in entire forgetfulness,
And not in utter nakedness,
But trailing clouds of glory do we come
From God, who is our home:
Heaven lies about us in our infancy!
Shades of the prison-house begin to close
Upon the growing Boy,
But he beholds the light, and whence it flows,
He sees it in his joy;
The Youth, who daily farther from the east
Must travel, still is Nature's priest,
And by the vision splendid
Is on his way attended;
At length the Man perceives it die away,
And fade into the light of common day.

VI

Earth fills her lap with pleasures of her own;
Yearnings she hath in her own natural kind,
And, even with something of a mother's mind,
And no unworthy aim,
The homely nurse doth all she can
To make her foster-child, her inmate, Man,
Forget the glories he hath known,
And that imperial palace whence he came.

VII

Behold the Child among his new-born blisses,
A six years' darling of a pigmy size!
See, where 'mid work of his own hand he lies,
Fretted by sallies of his mother's kisses,
With light upon him from his father's eyes!
See, at his feet, some little plan or chart,
Some fragment from his dream of human life,
Shaped by himself with newly-learned art;
A wedding or a festival,
A mourning or a funeral;
And this hath now his heart,
And unto this he frames his song:
Then will he fit his tongue
To dialogues of business, love, or strife;
But it will not be long
Ere this be thrown aside,
And with new joy and pride

The little actor cons another part;
Filling from time to time his 'humorous stage'
With all the Persons, down to palsied Age,
That life brings with her in her equipage;
As if his whole vocation
Were endless imitation.

VIII

Thou, whose exterior semblance doth belie
Thy soul's immensity;
Thou best philosopher, who yet dost keep
Thy heritage, thou eye among the blind,
That, deaf and silent, read'st the eternal deep,
Haunted for ever by the eternal Mind,–
Mighty Prophet! Seer blest!
On whom those truths rest
Which we are toiling all our lives to find,
In darkness lost, the darkness of the grave;
Thou, over whom thy Immortality
Broods like the day, a master o'er a slave,
A Presence which is not to be put by;
Thou little child, yet glorious in the might
Of heaven-born freedom on thy being's height,
Why with such earnest pains dost thou provoke
The years to bring the inevitable yoke,
Thus blindly with thy blessedness at strife?
Full soon thy soul shall have her earthly freight,
And custom lie upon thee with a weight
Heavy as frost, and deep almost as life!

IX

O joy! that in our embers
Is something that doth live,
That Nature yet remembers
What was so fugitive!
The thought of our past years in me doth breed
Perpetual benediction: not indeed
For that which is most worthy to be blest,
Delight and liberty, the simple creed
Of Childhood, whether busy or at rest,
With new-fledged hope still fluttering in his breast:–
– Not for these I raise
The song of thanks and praise;
But for those obstinate questionings
Of sense and outward things,
Failings from us, vanishings,
Blank misgivings of a creature
Moving about in worlds not realized,
High instincts, before which our mortal nature
Did tremble like a guilty thing surprised:
But for those first affections,
Those shadowy recollections,
Which, be they what they may,
Are yet the fountain-light of all our day,
Are yet a master-light of all our seeing;
Uphold us – cherish – and have power to make
Our noisy years seem moments in the being
Of the eternal Silence: truths that wake,

To perish never;
Which neither listlessness, nor mad endeavour,
Nor man nor boy,
Nor all that is at enmity with joy,
Can utterly abolish or destroy!
Hence, in a season of calm weather
Though inland far we be,
Our souls have sight of that immortal sea
Which brought us hither;
Can in a moment travel thither –
And see the children sport upon the shore,
And hear the mighty waters rolling evermore.

X

Then, sing, ye birds, sing, sing a joyous song!
And let the young lambs bound
As to the tabor's sound!
We, in thought, will join your throng,
Ye that pipe and ye that play,
Ye that through your hearts to-day
Feel the gladness of the May!
What though the radiance which was once so bright
Be now for ever taken from my sight,
Though nothing can bring back the hour
Of splendour in the grass, of glory in the flower;
We will grieve not, rather find
Strength in what remains behind;
In the primal sympathy

Which having been must ever be;
In the soothing thoughts that spring
Out of human suffering;
In the faith that looks through death,
In years that bring the philosophic mind.

XI

And O, ye Fountains, Meadows, Hills, and Groves,
Forebode not any severing of our loves!
Yet in my heart of hearts I feel your might;
I only have relinquish'd one delight
To live beneath your more habitual sway;
I love the brooks which down their channels fret
Even more than when I tripp'd lightly as they;
The innocent brightness of a new-born day
Is lovely yet;
The clouds that gather round the setting sun
Do take a sober colouring from an eye
That hath kept watch o'er man's mortality;
Another race hath been, and other palms are won.
Thanks to the human heart by which we live,
Thanks to its tenderness, its joys, and fears,
To me the meanest flower that blows can give
Thoughts that do often lie too deep for tears.

– Home at Grasmere, from *The Recluse* (1806) –

On Nature's invitation do I come,
By Reason sanctioned. Can the choice mislead,
That made the calmest, fairest spot of earth,
With all its unappropriated good,
My own, and not mine only, for with me
Entrenched – say rather peacefully embowered –
Under yon orchard, in yon humble cot,
A younger orphan of a home extinct,
The only daughter of my parents dwells:
   Aye, think on that, my heart, and cease to stir;
Pause upon that, and let the breathing frame
No longer breathe, but all be satisfied.
– Oh, if such silence be not thanks to God
For what hath been bestowed, then where, where then
Shall gratitude find rest? Mine eyes did ne'er
Fix on a lovely object, nor my mind
Take pleasure in the midst of happy thoughts,
But either she, whom now I have, who now
Divides with me this loved abode, was there,
Or not far off. Where'er my footsteps turned,
Her voice was like a hidden bird that sang;
The thought of her was like a flash of light
Or an unseen companionship, a breath
Or fragrance independent of the wind.
In all my goings, in the new and old
Of all my meditations, and in this

Favourite of all, in this the most of all
– What being, therefore, since the birth of Man
Had ever more abundant cause to speak
Thanks, and if favours of the Heavenly Muse
Make him more thankful, then to call on Verse
To aid him and in song resound his joy?
The boon is absolute; surpassing grace
To me hath been vouchsafed; among the bowers
Of blissful Eden this was neither given
Nor could be given, possession of the good
Which had been sighed for, ancient thought fulfilled,
And dear Imaginations realised,
Up to their highest measure, yea and more.

    Embrace me then, ye hills, and close me in.
Now in the clear and open day I feel
Your guardianship: I take it to my heart;
'Tis like the solemn shelter of the night.
But I would call thee beautiful; for mild,
And soft, and gay, and beautiful thou art,
Dear valley, having in thy face a smile,
Though peaceful, full of gladness. Thou art pleased,
Pleased with thy crags, and woody steeps, thy lake,
Its one green island, and its winding shores,
The multitude of little rocky hills,
Thy church, and cottages of mountain-stone
Clustered like stars some few, but single most,
And lurking dimly in their shy retreats,
Or glancing at each other cheerful looks,
Like separated stars with clouds between.

– Composed by the Side of Grasmere Lake
(1807) –

Clouds, lingering yet, extend in solid bars
Through the grey west; and lo! these waters, steeled
By breezeless air to smoothest polish, yield
A vivid repetition of the stars;
Jove, Venus, and the ruddy crest of Mars
Amid his fellows beauteously revealed
At happy distance from earth's groaning field,
Where ruthless mortals wage incessant wars.
Is it a mirror? or the nether Sphere
Opening to view the abyss in which she feeds
Her own calm fires? But list! a voice is near;
Great Pan himself low-whispering through the
    reeds,
'Be thankful, thou; for, if unholy deeds
Ravage the world, tranquillity is here!'

– The Solitary Reaper (1807) –

Behold her, single in the field,
Yon solitary Highland Lass!
Reaping and singing by herself;
Stop here, or gently pass!
Alone she cuts and binds the grain,
And sings a melancholy strain;
O listen! for the Vale profound
Is overflowing with the sound.

No Nightingale did ever chaunt
More welcome notes to weary bands
Of travellers in some shady haunt,
Among Arabian sands:
A voice so thrilling ne'er was heard
In spring-time from the Cuckoo-bird,
Breaking the silence of the seas
Among the farthest Hebrides.

Will no one tell me what she sings? –
Perhaps the plaintive numbers flow
For old, unhappy, far-off things,
And battles long ago:
Or is it some more humble lay,
Familiar matter of to-day?
Some natural sorrow, loss, or pain,
That has been, and may be again?

Whate'er the theme, the Maiden sang
As if her song could have no ending;
I saw her singing at her work,
And o'er the sickle bending; –
I listened, motionless and still;
And, as I mounted up the hill,
The music in my heart I bore,
Long after it was heard no more.

– The Sparrow's Nest (1807) –

Behold, within the leafy shade,
Those bright blue eggs together laid!
On me the chance-discovered sight
Gleamed like a vision of delight.
I started – seeming to espy
The home and sheltered bed,
The Sparrow's dwelling, which, hard by
My Father' house, in wet or dry
My sister Emmeline and I
    Together visited.

She looked at it and seemed to fear it;
Dreading, tho' wishing, to be near it:
Such heart was in her, being then
A little Prattler among men.
The Blessing of my later year
Was with me when a boy:
She gave me eyes, she gave me ears;
And humble care, and delicate fears;
A heart, the fountain of sweet tears;
    And love, and thought, and joy.

– To a Butterfly (1807) –

Stay near me – do not take thy flight!
A little longer stay in sight!
Much converse do I find I thee,
Historian of my infancy!
Float near me; do not yet depart!
Dead times revive in thee:
Thou bring'st, gay creature as thou art!
A solemn image to my heart,
My father's family!

Oh! pleasant, pleasant were the days,
The time, when, in our childish plays,
My sister Emmeline and I
Together chased the butterfly!
A very hunter did I rush
Upon the prey: – with leaps and spring
I followed on from brake to bush;
But she, God love her, feared to brush
The dust from off its wings.

– My Heart Leaps Up When I Behold (1807) –

My heart leaps up when I behold
A rainbow in the sky:
So was it when my life began;
So is it now I am a man;
So be it when I shall grow old,
Or let me die!
The Child is father of the Man;
And I could wish my days to be
Bound each to each by natural piety.

– Yew-Trees (1815) –

There is a Yew-tree, pride of Lorton Vale,
Which to this day stands single, in the midst
Of its own darkness, as it stood of yore:
Not loathe to furnish weapons for the Bands
Of Umfraville or Percy ere they marched
To Scotland's heaths; or those that crossed the sea
And drew their sounding bows at Azincour,
Perhaps at earlier Crecy, or Poictiers.
Of vast circumference and gloom profound
This solitary Tree! – a living thing
Produced too slowly ever to decay;
Of form and aspect too magnificent
To be destroyed. But worthier still of note
Are those fraternal Four of Borrowdale,
Joined in one solemn and capacious grove;
Huge trunks! – and each particular trunk a growth
Of intertwisted fibres serpentine
Up-coiling, and inveteratley convolved, –
Nor uninformed with Fantasy, and looks
That threaten the profane; – a pillared shade,
Upon whose grassless floor of red-brown hue,
By sheddings from the pining umbrage tinged
Perennially – beneath whose sable roof
Of boughs, as if for festal purpose decked
With unrejoicing berries – ghostly Shapes
May meet at noontide: Fear and trembling Hope,
Silence and Foresight, Death the Skeleton

And Time the Shadow; there to celebrate,
As in a natural temple scattered o'er
With altars undisturbed of mossy stone,
United worship; or in mute repose
To lie, and listen to the mountain flood
Murmuring from Glaramara's inmost caves.

– Airey-Force Valley (1836) –

– Not a breath of air
Ruffles the bosom of this leafy glen.
From the brook's margin, wide around, the trees
Are stedfast as the rocks; the brook itself,
Old as the hills that feed it from afar,
Doth rather deepen than disturb the calm
Where all things else are still and motionless.
And yet, even now, a little breeze, perchance
Escaped from boisterous winds that rage without,
Has entered, by the sturdy oaks unfelt,
But to its gentle touch how sensitive
Is the light ash! that, pendent from the brow
Of yon dim cave, in seeming silence makes
A soft eye-music of slow-waving boughs,
Powerful almost as vocal harmony
To stay the wanderer's steps and soothe his thoughts.

DOROTHY WORDSWORTH
(1771–1885)

D orothy Mae Ann Wordsworth was an English poet and
diarist whose *Alfoxden Journal* (1798) and *Grasmere
Journals* (1800–1803) are read today for the imaginative power
of their descriptions of nature and for the light they throw on
her brother, William Wordsworth, and Samuel Taylor Col-
eridge. The third of five children who were orphaned at an
early age, Dorothy was sent away to live with relatives and
was separated from her brothers. Nine years later, when she
moved into her grandparents' house in Penrith and was reu-
nited with them, she discovered, in William Wordsworth, a
soulmate. They lived together for many years, in Dorset, Som-
erset (near Samuel Taylor Coleridge), in Germany and finally
at Dove Cottage, Grasmere and Rydal Mount in the Lake
District. A handful of poems were published anonymously
in her lifetime, but none of her prose was for she did not view
herself as a writer and did not actively seek to publish her
work, but the material in her *Journals*, including descriptions
of nature, landscapes and seasons written after long walks in
the Lake District, were mined by William Wordsworth and
his contemporaries to the extent that they are now considered
to be not only examples of some of the strongest Romantic
writing of the day, but also to be a significant part of the lit-
erature of the Lake Poets. For instance, the *Grasmere Jour-
nals* contains a description of daffodils that inspired William
Wordsworth's famous poem 'I Wander'd Lonely as a Cloud'.

– *from* Grasmere Journals (1802) –

[April] 15th, Thursday. It was a threatening, misty morning, but mild. We set off after dinner from Eusemere. Mrs Clarkson went a short way with us but turned back. The wind was furious and we thought we must have returned. We first rested in the large boat-house, then under a furze bush opposite Mr Clarkson's. Saw the plough going in the field. The wind seized our breath. The Lake was rough. There was a boat by itself floating in the middle of the bay below Water Millock. We rested again in the Water Millock Lane. The hawthorns are black and green, the birches here and there greenish but there is yet more of purple to be seen on the twigs. We got over into a field to avoid some cows – people working. A few primroses by the roadside, wood-sorrel flower, the anemone, scentless violets, strawberries, and that starry yellow flower which Mrs C. calls pile wort. When we were in the woods beyond Gowbarrow park we saw a few daffodils close to the water-side. We fancied that the lake had floated the seeds ashore and that the little colony had so sprung up. But as we went along there were more and yet more; and at last, under the boughs of the trees, we saw that there was a long belt of them along the shore, about the breadth of a country turnpike road. I never saw daffodils so beautiful. They grew among the mossy stones about and about them,

some rested their heads upon these stones as on a pillow for weariness and the rest tossed and reeled and danced, and seemed as if they verily laughed with the wind, that blew upon them over the lake; they looked so gay, ever glancing, ever changing. This wind blew directly over the lake to them. There was here and there a little knot and a few stragglers a few yards higher up but they were so few as not to disturb the simplicity and unity and life of that one busy highway. We rested again and again. The bays were stormy, and we heard the waves at different distances and in the middle of the water like the sea. Rain came on – we were wet when we reached Luffs but we called in. Luckily all was cheerless and gloomy so we faced the storm – we *must* have been wet if we had waited – put on dry clothes at Dobson's. I was very kindly treated by a young woman, the Landlady looked sour but it is her way. She gave us a goodish supper. Excellent ham and potatoes. We paid 7/– when we came away. William was sitting by a bright fire when I came downstairs. He soon made his way to the library piled up in a corner of the window. He brought out a volume of Enfield's *Speaker*, another miscellany, and an odd volume of Congreve's plays. We had a glass of warm rum and water. We enjoyed ourselves and wished for Mary. It rained and blew when we went to bed. N.B. Deer in Gowbarrow park like skeletons.

April 16th, Friday (Good Friday). When I undrew curtains in the morning, I was much affected by the beauty of the prospect, and the change. The sun shone, the wind had passed away, the hills looked cheerful, the river was very bright as it flowed into the lake. The church rises up behind a little knot of rocks, the steeple not so high as an ordinary three-story house. Trees in a row in the garden under the wall. The valley is at first broken by little woody knolls that make retiring places, fairy valleys in the vale, the river winds along under these hills, travelling, not in a bustle but not slowly, to the lake. We saw a fisherman in the flat meadow on the other side of the water. He came towards us, and threw his line over the two-arched bridge. It is a bridge of a heavy construction, almost bending inwards in the middle, but it is grey, and there is a look of ancientry in the architecture of it that pleased me. As we go on the vale opens out more into one vale, with somewhat of a cradle bed. Cottages, with groups of trees, on the side of the hills. We passed a pair of twin children, two years old. Sate on the next bridge which we crossed – a single arch. We rested again upon the turf, and looked at the same bridge. We observed arches in the water, occasioned by the large stones sending it down in two streams. A sheep came plunging through the river, stumbled up the bank, and passed close to us. It had been frightened by an insignificant little dog on the other side. Its fleece dropped a glittering shower under its belly. Prim-roses by the road-side, pile wort that shone like stars of gold in the sun, violets, strawberries, retired and half-buried among the grass. When we came to the foot of Brothers Water, I left William sitting on the bridge, and went along the path on the right side of the lake through the wood. I was delighted with what I saw. The water under the boughs of the bare old trees, the simplicity of the mountains, and the exquisite beauty of the path. There was one grey cot-tage. I repeated *The Glow-worm*, as I walked along. I hung over the gate, and thought I could have stayed for ever. When I returned, I found William writing a poem descriptive of the sights and sounds we saw and heard. There was the gentle flowing of the stream, the glittering, lively lake, green fields without a living creature to be seen on them; behind us, a flat pasture with forty-two cattle feeding; to our left, the road leading to the hamlet. No smoke there, the sun shone on the bare roofs. The people were at work ploughing, harrowing, and sowing; . . . a dog barking now and then, cocks crowing, birds twittering, the snow in patches at the top of the highest hills, yellow palms, purple and green twigs on the birches, ashes with their glittering stems quite bare. The hawthorn a bright green, with black stems under the oak. The moss of the oak glossy. We went on. Passed two sisters at work (they first passed us), one with two pitchforks in her hand, the other had a spade. We had come to talk with them. They laughed long after we were gone, perhaps half in wantonness, half boldness. William finished his poem. Before we got to the foot of Kirkstone, there were hundreds of cattle in the vale. There we ate our dinner. The walk up Kirkstone was very interesting. The becks among the rocks were all alive. William showed me the little mossy streamlet which he had before loved when he saw its bright green track in the snow. The view above Ambleside very beautiful. There we sate and looked down on the green vale. We watched the crows at a little distance from us become white as silver as they flew in the sunshine, and when they went still further, they looked like shapes of water passing over the green fields. The whitening of Ambleside church is a great deduction from the beauty of it, seen from this point. We called at the Luffs, the Roddingtons there. Did not go in, and went round by the fields. I pulled off my stockings, intending to wade the beck, but I was obliged to put them on, and we climbed over the wall at the bridge. The post passed us. No letters. Rydale Lake was in its own evening brightness: the Island, and Points distinct. Jane Ashburner came up to us when we were sitting upon the wall . . . The garden looked pretty in the half-moonlight, half-daylight, as we went up the vale . . .

– Floating Island at Hawkshead, An Incident in the Schemes of Nature (*c.*1820s) –

Harmonious Powers with Nature work
On sky, earth, river, lake, and sea:
Sunshine and storm, whirlwind and breeze
All in one duteous task agree.

Once did I see a slip of earth,
By throbbing waves long undermined,
Loosed from its hold; – how no one knew
But all might see it float, obedient to the wind.

Might see it, from the mossy shore
Dissevered float upon the Lake,
Float, with its crest of trees adorned
On which the warbling birds their pastime take.

Food, shelter, safety there they find
There berries ripen, flowerets bloom;
There insects live their lives – and die:
A peopled world it is; in size a tiny room.

And thus through many seasons' space
This little Island may survive
But Nature, though we mark her not,
Will take away – may cease to give.

Perchance when you are wandering forth
Upon some vacant sunny day

Without an object, hope, or fear,
Thither your eyes may turn – the Isle is passed
    away.

Buried beneath the glittering Lake!
Its place no longer to be found,
Yet the lost fragments shall remain,
To fertilize some other ground.

– Thoughts on My Sick-Bed (*c.*1832) –

And has the remnant of my life
Been pilfered of this sunny Spring?
And have its own prelusive sounds
Touched in my heart no echoing string?

Ah! Say not so – the hidden life
Couchant within this feeble frame
Hath been enriched by kindred gifts,
That, undesired, unsought-for, came

With joyful heart in youthful days
When fresh each season in its Round
I welcomed the earliest Celandine
Glittering upon the mossy ground;

With busy eyes I pierced the lane
In quest of known and *un*known things,

– The primrose a lamp on its fortress rock,
The silent butterfly spreading its wings,

The violet betrayed by its noiseless breath,
The daffodil dancing in the breeze,
The carolling thrush, on his naked perch,
Towering above the budding trees.

Our cottage-hearth no longer our home,
Companions of Nature were we,
The Stirring, the Still, the Loquacious, the Mute –
To all we gave our sympathy.

Yet never in those careless days
When spring-time in rock, field, or bower
Was but a fountain of earthly hope
 A promise of fruits & the *splendid* flower.

No! then I never felt a bliss
That might with *that* compare
Which, piercing to my couch of rest,
Came on the vernal air.

When loving Friends an offering brought,
The first flowers of the year,
Culled from the precincts of our home,
From nooks to Memory dear.

With some sad thoughts the work was done.
Unprompted and unbidden,
But joy it brought to my *hidden* life,
To consciousness no longer hidden.

I felt a Power unfelt before,
Controlling weakness, languor, pain;
It bore me to the Terrace walk
I trod the Hills again; –

No prisoner in this lonely room,
I *saw* the green Banks of the Wye,
Recalling thy prophetic words,
Bard, Brother, Friend from infancy!

No need of motion, or of strength,
Or even the breathing air;
– I thought of Nature's loveliest scenes;
And with Memory I was there.

– Grasmere: A Fragment (1892) –

Peaceful our valley, fair and green,
And beautiful her cottages,
Each in its nook, its sheltered hold,
Or underneath its tuft of trees.

Many and beautiful they are;
But there is *one* that I love best,
A lowly shed, in truth, it is,
A brother of the rest.

Yet when I sit on rock or hill,
Down looking on the valley fair,

That Cottage with its clustering trees
Summons my heart; it settles there.

Others there are whose small domain
Of fertile fields and hedgerows green
Might more seduce a wanderer's mind
To wish that *there* his home had been.

Such wish be his! I blame him not,
My fancies they perchance are wild
– I love that house because it is
The very Mountains' child.

Fields hath it of its own, green fields,
But they are rocky steep and bare;
Their fence is of the mountain stone,
And moss and lichen flourish there.
And when the storm comes from the North
It lingers near that pastoral spot,
And, piping through the mossy walls,
It seems delighted with its lot.

And let it take its own delight;
And let it range the pastures bare;
Until it reach that group of trees,
– It may not enter there!

A green unfading grove it is,
Skirted with many a lesser tree,
Hazel and holly, beech and oak,
A bright and flourishing company.

Precious the shelter of those trees;
They screen the cottage that I love;
The sunshine pierces to the roof,
And the tall pine-trees tower above.

When first I saw that dear abode,
It was a lovely winter's day:
After a night of perilous storm
The west wind ruled with gentle sway;

A day so mild, it might have been
The first day of the gladsome spring;
The robins warbled, and I heard
One solitary throstle sing.

A Stranger, Grasmere, in thy Vale,
All faces then to me unknown,
I left my sole companion-friend
To wander out alone.

Lured by a little winding path,
I quitted soon the public road,
A smooth and tempting path it was,
By sheep and shepherds trod.

Eastward, toward the lofty hills,
This pathway led me on
Until I reached a stately Rock,
With velvet moss o'ergrown.

With russet oak and tufts of fern
Its top was richly garlanded;

Its sides adorned with eglantine
Bedropp'd with hips of glossy red.

There, too, in many a sheltered chink
The foxglove's broad leaves flourished fair,
And silver birch whose purple twigs
Bend to the softest breathing air.

Beneath that Rock my course I stayed,
And, looking to its summit high,
'Thou wear'st,' said I, 'a splendid garb,
Here winter keeps his revelry.

Full long a dweller on the Plains,
I griev'd when summer days were gone;
No more I'll grieve; for Winter here
Hath pleasure gardens of his own.
What need of flowers? The splendid moss
Is gayer than an April mead;
More rich its hues of various green,
Orange, and gold, & glittering red.'

– Beside that gay and lovely Rock
There came with merry voice
A foaming streamlet glancing by;
It seemed to say 'Rejoice!'

My youthful wishes all fulfill'd,
Wishes matured by thoughtful choice,
I stood an Inmate of this vale
How *could* I but rejoice?

– To D (*c*.1897) –

A thousand delicate fibres link
My heart in love to thee dear Maid
Though thine be youth's rejoicing prime
My lively vigour long decayed

Thou art a native of these hills
And their prized nursling still hast been
And thou repay'st their fostering love
As testify thy happy looks, thy graceful joyous
    mien.

This mountain land delights us both
We love each rocky hill;
I hither came in age mature
With thoughtful choice and placid Will.

And I have found the peace I sought
Which thou unsought hast found.

SAMUEL TAYLOR COLERIDGE
(1772–1834)

Samuel Taylor Coleridge was an English poet, literary critic, philosopher and theologian who – along with Wordsworth – was a founder of the Romantic movement in England. He also collaborated with Charles Lamb, Robert Southey and Charles Lloyd. Born in Ottery St Mary, Devon, Coleridge was the youngest of fourteen children. He was educated in London and at Cambridge University and found fame as a public lecturer and philosopher after graduation. In 1795, he married Sarah Fricker, whose sister was married to his friend, the writer Robert Southey. In that same year, while living in Somerset, he met William and Dorothy Wordsworth, which was the start of their famous literary collaboration. In 1789, Coleridge and the Wordsworths travelled to Germany and on his return, Coleridge settled in Greta Hall, Keswick, to be close to the William and Dorothy, who were now living in Grasmere. As his marriage fell apart, Coleridge often stayed with the Wordsworths, but he was a difficult houseguest as his addiction to laudanum grew and his frequent nightmares would wake the children. He was also a fussy eater, to the frustration of Dorothy, who had to cook, and he became infatuated with Wordsworth's sister-in-law, Sara Hutchinson. The pair fell out in 1810, but made up later in life. Coleridge is responsible for some of the best-known poems in the English language, including 'The Rime of the Ancient Mariner', 'Kubla Khan' and 'Frost at Midnight'. Coleridge died in London in July 1834 and is buried in St Michael's Church, Highgate.

– The Eolian Harp (1796) –

My pensive Sara! thy soft cheek reclined
Thus on mine arm, most soothing sweet it is
To sit beside our Cot, our Cot o'ergrown
With white-flowered Jasmin, and the broad-leaved
    Myrtle,
(Meet emblems they of Innocence and Love!)
And watch the clouds, that late were rich with
    light,
Slow saddening round, and mark the star of eve
Serenely brilliant (such would Wisdom be)
Shine opposite! How exquisite the scents
Snatched from yon bean-field! and the world so
    hushed!
The stilly murmur of the distant Sea
Tells us of silence.

               And that simplest Lute,
Placed length-ways in the clasping casement, hark!
How by the desultory breeze caressed,
Like some coy maid half yielding to her lover,
It pours such sweet upbraiding, as must needs
Tempt to repeat the wrong! And now, its strings
Boldlier swept, the long sequacious notes
Over delicious surges sink and rise,
Such a soft floating witchery of sound
As twilight Elfins make, when they at eve
Voyage on gentle gales from Fairy-Land,

Where Melodies round honey-dropping flowers,
Footless and wild, like birds of Paradise,
Nor pause, nor perch, hovering on untamed wing!
O! the one Life within us and abroad,
Which meets all motion and becomes its soul,
A light in sound, a sound-like power in light,
Rhythm in all thought, and joyance everywhere –
Methinks, it should have been impossible
Not to love all things in a world so filled;
Where the breeze warbles, and the mute still air
Is Music slumbering on her instrument.

And thus, my Love! as on the midway slope
Of yonder hill I stretch my limbs at noon,
Whilst through my half-closed eyelids I behold
The sunbeams dance, like diamonds, on the main,
And tranquil muse upon tranquility:
Full many a thought uncalled and undetained,
And many idle flitting phantasies,
Traverse my indolent and passive brain,
As wild and various as the random gales
That swell and flutter on this subject Lute!

And what if all of animated nature
Be but organic Harps diversely framed,
That tremble into thought, as o'er them sweeps
Plastic and vast, one intellectual breeze,
At once the Soul of each, and God of all?

But thy more serious eye a mild reproof

Darts, O beloved Woman! nor such thoughts
Dim and unhallowed dost thou not reject,
And biddest me walk humbly with my God.
Meek Daughter in the family of Christ!
Well hast thou said and holily dispraised
These shapings of the unregenerate mind;
Bubbles that glitter as they rise and break
On vain Philosophy's aye-babbling spring.
For never guiltless may I speak of him,
The Incomprehensible! save when with awe
I praise him, and with Faith that inly *feels*;
Who with his saving mercies healed me,
A sinful and most miserable man,
Wildered and dark, and gave me to possess
Peace, and this Cot, and thee, heart-honored Maid!

– To the River Otter (1796) –

Dear native brook! wild streamlet of the West!
How many various-fated years have passed,
What happy and what mournful hours, since last
I skimmed the smooth thin stone along thy breast,
Numbering its light leaps! Yet so deep impressed
Sink the sweet scenes of childhood, that mine eyes
I never shut amid the sunny ray,
But straight with all their tints thy waters rise,
Thy crossing plank, thy marge with willows grey,
And bedded sand that, veined with various dyes,
Gleamed through thy bright transparence!
On my way, Visions of childhood! oft have ye
    beguiled
Lone manhood's cares, yet waking fondest sighs:
Ah! that once more I were a careless child!

– This Lime-tree Bower My Prison (1797) –

[Addressed to Charles Lamb, of the India House, London]

Well, they are gone, and here must I remain,
This lime-tree bower my prison! I have lost
Beauties and feelings, such as would have been
Most sweet to my remembrance even when age
Had dimm'd mine eyes to blindness! They, meanwhile,
Friends, whom I never more may meet again,
On springy heath, along the hill-top edge,
Wander in gladness, and wind down, perchance,
To that still roaring dell, of which I told;
The roaring dell, o'erwooded, narrow, deep,
And only speckled by the mid-day sun;
Where its slim trunk the ash from rock to rock
Flings arching like a bridge; – that branchless ash,
Unsunn'd and damp, whose few poor yellow leaves
Ne'er tremble in the gale, yet tremble still,
Fann'd by the water-fall! and there my friends
Behold the dark green file of long lank weeds,
That all at once (a most fantastic sight!)
Still nod and drip beneath the dripping edge
Of the blue clay-stone.

                              Now, my friends emerge
Beneath the wide wide Heaven – and view again
The many-steepled tract magnificent
Of hilly fields and meadows, and the sea,

With some fair bark, perhaps, whose sails light up
The slip of smooth clear blue betwixt two Isles
Of purple shadow! Yes! they wander on
In gladness all; but thou, methinks, most glad,
My gentle-hearted Charles! for thou hast pined
And hunger'd after Nature, many a year,
In the great City pent, winning thy way
With sad yet patient soul, through evil and pain
And strange calamity! Ah! slowly sink
Behind the western ridge, thou glorious Sun!
Shine in the slant beams of the sinking orb,
Ye purple heath-flowers! richlier burn, ye clouds!
Live in the yellow light, ye distant groves!
And kindle, thou blue Ocean! So my friend
Struck with deep joy may stand, as I have stood,
Silent with swimming sense; yea, gazing round
On the wide landscape, gaze till all doth seem
Less gross than bodily; and of such hues
As veil the Almighty Spirit, when yet he makes
Spirits perceive his presence.

                      A delight
Comes sudden on my heart, and I am glad
As I myself were there! Nor in this bower,
This little lime-tree bower, have I not mark'd
Much that has sooth'd me. Pale beneath the blaze
Hung the transparent foliage; and I watch'd
Some broad and sunny leaf, and lov'd to see
The shadow of the leaf and stem above

Dappling its sunshine! And that walnut-tree
Was richly ting'd, and a deep radiance lay
Full on the ancient ivy, which usurps
Those fronting elms, and now, with blackest mass
Makes their dark branches gleam a lighter hue
Through the late twilight: and though now the bat
Wheels silent by, and not a swallow twitters,
Yet still the solitary humble-bee
Sings in the bean-flower! Henceforth I shall know
That Nature ne'er deserts the wise and pure;
No plot so narrow, be but Nature there,
No waste so vacant, but may well employ
Each faculty of sense, and keep the heart
Awake to Love and Beauty! and sometimes
'Tis well to be bereft of promis'd good,
That we may lift the soul, and contemplate
With lively joy the joys we cannot share.
My gentle-hearted Charles! when the last rook
Beat its straight path along the dusky air
Homewards, I blest it! deeming its black wing
(Now a dim speck, now vanishing in light)
Had cross'd the mighty Orb's dilated glory,
While thou stood'st gazing; or, when all was still,
Flew creeking o'er thy head, and had a charm
For thee, my gentle-hearted Charles, to whom
No sound is dissonant which tells of Life.

– Frost at Midnight (1798) –

The Frost performs its secret ministry,
Unhelped by any wind. The owlet's cry
Came loud – and hark, again! loud as before.
The inmates of my cottage, all at rest,
Have left me to that solitude, which suits
Abstruser musings: save that at my side
My cradled infant slumbers peacefully.
'Tis calm indeed! so calm, that it disturbs
And vexes meditation with its strange
And extreme silentness. Sea, hill, and wood,
This populous village! Sea, and hill, and wood,
With all the numberless goings-on of life,
Inaudible as dreams! the thin blue flame
Lies on my low-burnt fire, and quivers not;
Only that film, which fluttered on the grate,

Still flutters there, the sole unquiet thing.
Methinks, its motion in this hush of nature
Gives it dim sympathies with me who live,
Making it a companionable form,
Whose puny flaps and freaks the idling Spirit
By its own moods interprets, every where
Echo or mirror seeking of itself,
And makes a toy of Thought.

                         But O! how oft,
How oft, at school, with most believing mind,
Presageful, have I gazed upon the bars,

To watch that fluttering *stranger*! and as oft
With unclosed lids, already had I dreamt
Of my sweet birth-place, and the old church-tower,
Whose bells, the poor man's only music, rang
From morn to evening, all the hot Fair-day,
So sweetly, that they stirred and haunted me
With a wild pleasure, falling on mine ear
Most like articulate sounds of things to come!
So gazed I, till the soothing things, I dreamt,
Lulled me to sleep, and sleep prolonged my dreams!
And so I brooded all the following morn,
Awed by the stern preceptor's face, mine eye
Fixed with mock study on my swimming book:
Save if the door half opened, and I snatched
A hasty glance, and still my heart leaped up,
For still I hoped to see the *stranger's* face,
Townsman, or aunt, or sister more beloved,
My play-mate when we both were clothed alike!

Dear Babe, that sleepest cradled by my side,
Whose gentle breathings, heard in this deep calm,
Fill up the intersperséd vacancies
And momentary pauses of the thought!
My babe so beautiful! it thrills my heart
With tender gladness, thus to look at thee,
And think that thou shalt learn far other lore,
And in far other scenes! For I was reared
In the great city, pent 'mid cloisters dim,
And saw nought lovely but the sky and stars.

But *thou*, my babe! shalt wander like a breeze
By lakes and sandy shores, beneath the crags
Of ancient mountain, and beneath the clouds,
Which image in their bulk both lakes and shores
And mountain crags: so shalt thou see and hear
The lovely shapes and sounds intelligible
Of that eternal language, which thy God
Utters, who from eternity doth teach
Himself in all, and all things in himself.
Great universal Teacher! he shall mould
Thy spirit, and by giving make it ask.

Therefore all seasons shall be sweet to thee,
Whether the summer clothe the general earth
With greenness, or the redbreast sit and sing
Betwixt the tufts of snow on the bare branch
Of mossy apple-tree, while the nigh thatch
Smokes in the sun-thaw; whether the eave-drops fall
Heard only in the trances of the blast,
Or if the secret ministry of frost
Shall hang them up in silent icicles,
Quietly shining to the quiet Moon.

– Fears in Solitude (1798) –

A green and silent spot, amid the hills,
A small and silent dell! O'er stiller place
No singing sky-lark ever poised himself.
The hills are heathy, save that swelling slope,
Which hath a gay and gorgeous covering on,
All golden with the never-bloomless furze,
Which now blooms most profusely; but the dell,
Bathed by the mist, is fresh and delicate
As vernal corn-field, or the unripe flax,
When, through its half-transparent stalks, at eve,
The level sunshine glimmers with green light.
Oh! 'tis a quiet spirit-healing nook!
Which all, methinks, would love; but chiefly he,
The humble man, who, in his youthful years,
Knew just so much of folly, as had made
His early manhood more securely wise!
Here he might lie on fern or withered heath,
While from the singing-lark (that sings unseen
The minstrelsy that solitude loves best),
And from the sun, and from the breezy air,
Sweet influences trembled o'er his frame;
And he, with many feelings, many thoughts,
Made up a meditative joy, and found
Religious meanings in the forms of nature!
And so, his senses gradually wrapt
In a half-sleep, he dreams of better worlds,
And dreaming hears thee still, O singing-lark;

That singest like an angel in the clouds!

        My God! it is a melancholy thing
For such a man, who would full fain preserve
His soul in calmness, yet perforce must feel
For all his human brethren – O my God!
It weighs upon the heart, that he must think
What uproar and what strife may now be stirring
This way or that way o'er these silent hills –
Invasion, and the thunder and the shout,
And all the crash of onset; fear and rage,
And undetermined conflict – even now,
Even now, perchance, and in his native isle:
Carnage and groans beneath this blessed sun!
We have offended, oh! my countrymen!
We have offended very grievously,
And been most tyrannous. From east to west
A groan of accusation pierces Heaven!
The wretched plead against us; multitudes
Countless and vehement, the sons of God,
Our brethren! Like a cloud that travels on,
Steamed up from Cairo's swamps of pestilence,
Even so, my countrymen! have we gone forth
And borne to distant tribes slavery and pangs,
And, deadlier far, our vices, whose deep taint
With slow perdition murders the whole man,
His body and his soul! Meanwhile, at home,
All individual dignity and power
Engulfed in courts, committees, institutions,

Associations and societies,
A vain, speech-mouthing, speech-reporting guild,
One benefit-club for mutual flattery,
We have drunk up, demure as at a grace,
Pollutions from the brimming cup of wealth;
Contemptuous of all honorable rule,
Yet bartering freedom and the poor man's life
For gold, as at a market! The sweet words
Of Christian promise, words that even yet
Might stem destruction, were they wisely preached,
Are muttered o'er by men, whose tones proclaim
How flat and wearisome they feel their trade:
Rank scoffers some, but most too indolent
To deem them falsehoods or to know their truth.
Oh! blasphemous! the book of life is made
A superstitious instrument, on which
We gabble o'er the oaths we mean to break;
For all must swear – all and in every place,
College and wharf, council and justice court;
All, all must swear, the briber and the bribed,
Merchant and lawyer, senator and priest,
The rich, the poor, the old man and the young;
All, all make up one scheme of perjury,
That faith doth reel; the very name of God
Sounds like a juggler's charm; and, bold with joy,
Forth from his dark and lonely hiding-place,
(Portentous sight!) the owlet Atheism,
Sailing on obscene wings athwart the noon,
Drops his blue-fringed lids, and holds them close,

And hooting at the glorious sun in Heaven,
Cries out, 'Where is it?'

                      Thankless too for peace
(Peace long preserved by fleets and perilous seas)
Secure from actual warfare, we have loved
To swell the war-whoop, passionate for war!
Alas! for ages ignorant of all
Its ghastlier workings (famine or blue plague,
Battle, or siege, or flight through wintry-snows),
We, this whole people, have been clamorous
For war and bloodshed; animating sports,
The which we pay for as a thing to talk of,
Spectators and not combatants! No guess
Anticipative of a wrong unfelt,
No speculation or contingency,
However dim and vague, too vague and dim
To yield a justifying cause; and forth
(Stuffed out with big preamble, holy names,
And adjurations of the God in Heaven,)
We send our mandates for the certain death
Of thousands and ten thousands! Boys and girls,
And women, that would groan to see a child
Pull off an insect's leg, all read of war,
The best amusement for our morning-meal!
The poor wretch, who has learnt his only prayers
From curses, who knows scarcely words enough
To ask a blessing from his Heavenly Father,
Becomes a fluent phraseman, absolute

And technical in victories and defeats,
And all our dainty terms for fratricide;
Terms which we trundle smoothly o'er our tongues
Like mere abstractions, empty sounds to which
We join no feeling and attach no form!
As if the soldier died without a wound;
As if the fibres of this godlike frame
Were gored without a pang; as if the wretch,
Who fell in battle, doing bloody deeds,
Passed off to Heaven, translated and not killed;
As though he had no wife to pine for him,
No God to judge him! Therefore, evil days
Are coming on us, O my countrymen!
And what if all-avenging Providence,
Strong and retributive, should make us know
The meaning of our words, force us to feel
The desolation and the agony
Of our fierce doings!

                 Spare us yet awhile,
Father and God! O! spare us yet awhile!
Oh! let not English women drag their flight
Fainting beneath the burthen of their babes,
Of the sweet infants, that but yesterday
Laughed at the breast! Sons, brothers, husbands, all
Who ever gazed with fondness on the forms
Which grew up with you round the same fire-side,
And all who ever heard the sabbath-bells
Without the infidel's scorn, make yourselves pure!

Stand forth! be men! repel an impious foe,
Impious and false, a light yet cruel race,
Who laugh away all virtue, mingling mirth
With deeds of murder; and still promising
Freedom, themselves too sensual to be free,
Poison life's amities, and cheat the heart
Of faith and quiet hope, and all that soothes
And all that lifts the spirit! Stand we forth;
Render them back upon the insulted ocean,
And let them toss as idly on its waves
As the vile sea-weed, which some mountain-blast
Swept from our shores! And oh! may we return
Not with a drunken triumph, but with fear,
Repenting of the wrongs with which we stung
So fierce a foe to frenzy!

                         I have told,
O Britons! O my brethren! I have told
Most bitter truth, but without bitterness.
Nor deem my zeal or factious or mis-timed;
For never can true courage dwell with them,
Who, playing tricks with conscience, dare not look
At their own vices. We have been too long
Dupes of a deep delusion! Some, belike,
Groaning with restless enmity, expect
All change from change of constituted power;
As if a Government had been a robe,
On which our vice and wretchedness were tagged
Like fancy-points and fringes, with the robe

Pulled off at pleasure. Fondly these attach
A radical causation to a few
Poor drudges of chastising Providence,
Who borrow all their hues and qualities
From our own folly and rank wickedness,
Which gave them birth and nursed them. Others,
    meanwhile,
Dote with a mad idolatry; and all
Who will not fall before their images,
And yield them worship, they are enemies
Even of their country!

          Such have I been deemed –
But, O dear Britain! O my Mother Isle!
Needs must thou prove a name most dear and holy
To me a son, a brother, and a friend.
A husband, and a father! who revere
All bonds of natural love, and find them all
Within the limits of thy rocky shores.
O native Britain! O my Mother Isle!
How shouldst thou prove aught else but dear and
    holy
To me, who from thy lakes and mountain-hills,
Thy clouds, thy quiet dales, thy rocks and seas,
Have drunk in all my intellectual life,
All sweet sensations, all ennobling thoughts,
All adoration of the God in nature,
All lovely and all honorable things,
Whatever makes this mortal spirit feel

The joy and greatness of its future being?
There lives nor form nor feeling in my soul
Unborrowed from my country. O divine
And beauteous island! thou hast been my sole
And most magnificent temple, in the which
I walk with awe, and sing my stately songs,
Loving the God that made me!

                    May my fears
My filial fears, be vain! and may the vaunts
And menace of the vengeful enemy
Pass like the gust, that roared and died away
In the distant tree: which heard, and only heard,
In this low dell, bowed not the delicate grass.

  But now the gentle dew-fall sends abroad
The fruit-like perfume of the golden furze:
The light has left the summit of the hill,
Though still a sunny gleam lies beautiful.
Aslant the ivied beacon. Now farewell,
Farewell, awhile, O soft and silent spot!
On the green sheep-track, up the heathy hill,
Homeward I wind my way; and lo! recalled
From bodings that have well-nigh wearied me,
I find myself upon the brow, and pause
Startled! And after lonely sojourning
In such a quiet and surrounded nook,
This burst of prospect, here the shadowy main,
Dim tinted, there the mighty majesty
Of that huge amphitheatre of rich

And elmy fields, seems like society --
Conversing with the mind, and giving it
A livelier impulse and a dance of thought!
And now, beloved Stowey! I behold
Thy church-tower, and, methinks, the four huge elms
Clustering, which mark the mansion of my friend;
And close behind them, hidden from my view,
Is my own lowly cottage, where my babe
And my babe's mother dwell in peace! With light
And quickened footsteps thitherward I tend,
Remembering thee, O green and silent dell!
And grateful, that by nature's quietness
And solitary musings, all my heart
Is softened, and made worthy to indulge
Love, and the thoughts that yearn for humankind.

– The Nightingale: A Conversation Poem
(1798) –

No cloud, no relique of the sunken day
Distinguishes the West, no long thin slip
Of sullen light, no obscure trembling hues.
Come, we will rest on this old mossy bridge!
You see the glimmer of the stream beneath,
But hear no murmuring: it flows silently.
O'er its soft bed of verdure. All is still.
A balmy night! and though the stars be dim,
Yet let us think upon the vernal showers
That gladden the green earth, and we shall find
A pleasure in the dimness of the stars.
And hark! the Nightingale begins its song,
'Most musical, most melancholy' bird!
A melancholy bird? Oh! idle thought!
In Nature there is nothing melancholy.
But some night-wandering man whose heart was
        pierced
With the remembrance of a grievous wrong,
Or slow distemper, or neglected love,
(And so, poor wretch! filled all things with himself,
And made all gentle sounds tell back the tale
Of his own sorrow) he, and such as he,
First named these notes a melancholy strain.
And many a poet echoes the conceit;
Poet who hath been building up the rhyme
When he had better far have stretched his limbs

Beside a brook in mossy forest-dell,
By sun or moon-light, to the influxes
Of shapes and sounds and shifting elements
Surrendering his whole spirit, of his song
And of his fame forgetful! so his fame
Should share in Nature's immortality,
A venerable thing! and so his song
Should make all Nature lovelier, and itself
Be loved like Nature! But 'twill not be so;
And youths and maidens most poetical,
Who lose the deepening twilights of the spring
In ball-rooms and hot theatres, they still
Full of meek sympathy must heave their sighs
O'er Philomela's pity-pleading strains.

My Friend, and thou, our Sister! we have learnt
A different lore: we may not thus profane
Nature's sweet voices, always full of love
And joyance! 'Tis the merry Nightingale
That crowds and hurries, and precipitates
With fast thick warble his delicious notes,
As he were fearful that an April night
Would be too short for him to utter forth
His love-chant, and disburthen his full soul
Of all its music!

                And I know a grove
Of large extent, hard by a castle huge,
Which the great lord inhabits not; and so
This grove is wild with tangling underwood,

And the trim walks are broken up, and grass,
Thin grass and king-cups grow within the paths.
But never elsewhere in one place I knew
So many nightingales; and far and near,
In wood and thicket, over the wide grove,
They answer and provoke each other's song,
With skirmish and capricious passagings,
And murmurs musical and swift jug jug,
And one low piping sound more sweet than all
Stirring the air with such a harmony,
That should you close your eyes, you might almost
Forget it was not day! On moonlight bushes,
Whose dewy leaflets are but half-disclosed,
You may perchance behold them on the twigs,
Their bright, bright eyes, their eyes both bright and
     full,
Glistening, while many a glow-worm in the shade
Lights up her love-torch.

                        A most gentle Maid,
Who dwelleth in her hospitable home
Hard by the castle, and at latest eve
(Even like a Lady vowed and dedicate
To something more than Nature in the grove)
Glides through the pathways; she knows all their
     notes,
That gentle Maid! and oft, a moment's space,
What time the moon was lost behind a cloud,
Hath heard a pause of silence; till the moon
Emerging, a hath awakened earth and sky

With one sensation, and those wakeful birds
Have all burst forth in choral minstrelsy,
As if some sudden gale had swept at once
A hundred airy harps! And she hath watched
Many a nightingale perch giddily
On blossomy twig still swinging from the breeze,
And to that motion tune his wanton song
Like tipsy Joy that reels with tossing head.

Farewell! O Warbler! till tomorrow eve,
And you, my friends! farewell, a short farewell!
We have been loitering long and pleasantly,
And now for our dear homes. That strain again!
Full fain it would delay me! My dear babe,
Who, capable of no articulate sound,
Mars all things with his imitative lisp,
How he would place his hand beside his ear,
His little hand, the small forefinger up,
And bid us listen! And I deem it wise
To make him Nature's play-mate. He knows well
The evening-star; and once, when he awoke
In most distressful mood (some inward pain
Had made up that strange thing, an infant's dream)
I hurried with him to our orchard-plot,
And he beheld the moon, and, hushed at once,
Suspends his sobs, and laughs most silently,
While his fair eyes, that swam with undropped tears,
Did glitter in the yellow moon-beam! Well!
It is a father's tale: But if that Heaven

Should give me life, his childhood shall grow up
Familiar with these songs, that with the night
He may associate joy. Once more, farewell,
Sweet Nightingale! once more, my friends! farewell.

– Letter to Josiah Wedgwood, Greta Hall, Thursday, 24 July, 1800 –

This is the first day of my arrival at Keswick – my house is roomy, situated on an eminence a furlong from the Town – before it an enormous Garden more than two thirds of which is rented as a Garden for sale articles, but the walks &c are our's most completely. Behind the house are shrubberies, & a declivity planted with flourishing trees of 15 years' growth or so, at the bottom of which is a most delightful shaded walk by the River Greta, a quarter of a mile in length. The room in which I sit, commands from one window the Basenthwaite Lake, Woods, & Mountains, from the opposite the Derwentwater & fantastic mountains of Borrowdale – straight before me is a wilderness of mountains, catching & streaming lights or shadows at all times – behind the house & entering into all our views is Skiddaw. My acquaintance here are pleasant – & at some distance is Sir Guilfrid Lawson's 1 Seat with a very large & expensive Library to which I have every reason to hope that I shall have free access. But when I have been settled here a few days longer, I will write you a minute account of my situation. Wordsworth lives 12 miles distant – in about a year's time he will probably settle at Keswick likewise. It is no small advantage here that for two thirds of the year we are in complete retirement – the other third is alive & swarms with Tourists of all shapes & sizes, & characters – it is the very place I would recommend to a novellist or farce writer. Besides, at that time of the year there is always hope that a friend may be among the number, & miscellaneous crowd, whom this place attracts. So much for Keswick at present.

– Inscription for a Seat by the Road Side (1800) –

. . . half-way up a steep hill facing south

Thou who in youthful vigour rich, and light
With youthful thoughts dost need no rest! O thou,
To whom alike the valley and the hill
Present a path of ease! Should e'er thine eye
Glance on this sod, and this rude tablet, stop!
'Tis a rude spot, yet here, with thankful hearts,
The foot-worn soldier and his family
Have rested, wife and babe, and boy, perchance

Some eight years old or less, and scantly fed,
Garbed like his father, and already bound
To his poor father's trade. Or think of him
Who, laden with his implements of toil,
Returns at night to some far distant home,
And having plodded on through rain and mire
With limbs o'erlaboured, weak from feverish heat,
And chafed and fretted by December blasts,
Here pauses, thankful he hath reached so far,
And 'mid the sheltering warmth of these bleak trees
Finds restoration – or reflect on those
Who in the spring to meet the warmer sun
Crawl up this steep hill-side, that needlessly
Bends double their weak frames, already bowed
By age or malady, and when, at last,
They gain this wished-for turf, this seat of sods,
Repose – and, well-admonished, ponder here
On final rest. And if a serious thought
Should come uncalled – how soon *thy* motions high,
Thy balmy spirits and thy fervid blood
Must change to feeble, withered, cold and dry,
Cherish the wholesome sadness! And where'er
The tide of Life impel thee, O be prompt
To make thy present strength the staff of all,
Their staff and resting-place – so shalt thou give
To Youth the sweetest joy that Youth can know;
And for thy future self thou shalt provide
Through every change of various life, a seat,
Not built by hands, on which thy inner part,

Imperishable, many a grievous hour,
Or bleak or sultry may repose – yea, sleep
The sleep of Death, and dream of blissful worlds,
Then wake in Heaven, and find the dream all true.

– A Stranger Minstrel (1801) –

Written to Mrs Robinson a few weeks before her death

As late on Skiddaw's mount I lay supine,
Midway th' ascent, in that repose divine
When the soul centred in the heart's recess
Hath quaff'd its fill of Nature's loveliness,
Yet still beside the fountain's marge will stay
And fain would thirst again, again to quaff;
Then when the tear, slow travelling on its way,
Fills up the wrinkles of a silent laugh –
In that sweet mood of sad and humorous thought
A form within me rose, within me wrought
With such strong magic, that I cried aloud,
'Thou ancient Skiddaw by thy helm of cloud,
And by thy many-colour'd chasms deep,
And by their shadows that for ever sleep,
By yon small flaky mists that love to creep
Along the edges of those spots of light,
Those sunny islands on thy smooth green height,
And by yon shepherds with their sheep,
And dogs and boys, a gladsome crowd,

That rush e'en now with clamour loud
Sudden from forth thy topmost cloud,
And by this laugh, and by this tear,
I would, old Skiddaw, she were here!
A lady of sweet song is she,
Her soft blue eye was made for thee!
O ancient Skiddaw, by this tear,
I would, I would that she were here!'

Then ancient Skiddaw, stern and proud,
In sullen majesty replying,
Thus spake from out his helm of cloud
(His voice was like an echo dying!): –
'She dwells belike in scenes more fair,
And scorns a mount so bleak and bare.'

I only sigh'd when this I heard,
Such mournful thoughts within me stirr'd
That all my heart was faint and weak,
So sorely was I troubled!
No laughter wrinkled on my cheek,
But O the tears were doubled!
But ancient Skiddaw green and high
Heard and understood my sigh;
And now, in tones less stern and rude,
As if he wish'd to end the feud,
Spake he, the proud response renewing
(His voice was like a monarch wooing): –
'Nay, but thou dost not know her might,
The pinions of her soul how strong!

But many a stranger in my height
Hath sung to me her magic song,
Sending forth his ecstasy
In her divinest melody,
And hence I know her soul is free,
She is where'er she wills to be,
Unfetter'd by mortality!
Now to the "haunted beach" can fly,
Beside the threshold scourged with waves,
Now where the maniac wildly raves,
"Pale moon, thou spectre of the sky!"
No wind that hurries o'er my height
Can travel with so swift a flight.
I too, methinks, might merit
The presence of her spirit!
To me too might belong
The honour of her song and witching melody,
Which most resembles me,
Soft, various, and sublime,
Exempt from wrongs of Time!'

Thus spake the mighty Mount, and I
Made answer, with a deep-drawn sigh: –
Thou ancient Skiddaw, by this tear,
I would, I would that she were here!'

– Dejection: An Ode (1802) –

Late, late yestreen I saw the new Moon,
With the old Moon in her arms;
And I fear, I fear, my Master dear!
We shall have a deadly storm.
    – *Ballad of Sir Patrick Spence*

I

Well! If the Bard was weather-wise, who made
   The grand old ballad of Sir Patrick Spence,
   This night, so tranquil now, will not go hence
Unroused by winds, that ply a busier trade
Than those which mould yon cloud in lazy flakes,
Or the dull sobbing draft, that moans and rakes
Upon the strings of this Æolian lute,
      Which better far were mute.
   For lo! the New-moon winter-bright!
   And overspread with phantom light,
   (With swimming phantom light o'erspread
   But rimmed and circled by a silver thread)
I see the old Moon in her lap, foretelling
   The coming-on of rain and squally blast.
And oh! that even now the gust were swelling,
   And the slant night-shower driving loud and fast!
Those sounds which oft have raised me, whilst they awed,
      And sent my soul abroad,
Might now perhaps their wonted impulse give,
Might startle this dull pain, and make it move and live!

II

A grief without a pang, void, dark, and drear,
    A stifled, drowsy, unimpassioned grief,
    Which finds no natural outlet, no relief,
        In word, or sigh, or tear –
O Lady! in this wan and heartless mood,
To other thoughts by yonder throstle woo'd,
    All this long eve, so balmy and serene,
Have I been gazing on the western sky,
    And its peculiar tint of yellow green:
And still I gaze – and with how blank an eye!
And those thin clouds above, in flakes and bars,
That give away their motion to the stars;
Those stars, that glide behind them or between,
Now sparkling, now bedimmed, but always seen:
Yon crescent Moon, as fixed as if it grew
In its own cloudless, starless lake of blue;
I see them all so excellently fair,
I see, not feel, how beautiful they are!

III

    My genial spirits fail;
    And what can these avail
To lift the smothering weight from off my breast?
    It were a vain endeavour,
    Though I should gaze for ever
On that green light that lingers in the west:
I may not hope from outward forms to win
The passion and the life, whose fountains are within.

IV

O Lady! we receive but what we give,
And in our life alone does Nature live:
Ours is her wedding garment, ours her shroud!
  And would we aught behold, of higher worth,
Than that inanimate cold world allowed
To the poor loveless ever-anxious crowd,
  Ah! from the soul itself must issue forth
A light, a glory, a fair luminous cloud
   Enveloping the Earth –
And from the soul itself must there be sent
  A sweet and potent voice, of its own birth,
Of all sweet sounds the life and element!

V

O pure of heart! thou need'st not ask of me
What this strong music in the soul may be!
What, and wherein it doth exist,
This light, this glory, this fair luminous mist,
This beautiful and beauty-making power.
  Joy, virtuous Lady! Joy that ne'er was given,
Save to the pure, and in their purest hour,
Life, and Life's effluence, cloud at once and shower,
Joy, Lady! is the spirit and the power,
Which wedding Nature to us gives in dower
  A new Earth and new Heaven,
Undreamt of by the sensual and the proud –
Joy is the sweet voice, Joy the luminous cloud –

We in ourselves rejoice!
And thence flows all that charms or ear or sight,
        All melodies the echoes of that voice,
All colours a suffusion from that light.

VI

There was a time when, though my path was rough,
        This joy within me dallied with distress,
And all misfortunes were but as the stuff
        Whence Fancy made me dreams of happiness:
For hope grew round me, like the twining vine,
And fruits, and foliage, not my own, seemed mine.
But now afflictions bow me down to earth:
Nor care I that they rob me of my mirth;
        But oh! each visitation
Suspends what nature gave me at my birth,
        My shaping spirit of Imagination.
For not to think of what I needs must feel,
        But to be still and patient, all I can;
And haply by abstruse research to steal
        From my own nature all the natural man –
        This was my sole resource, my only plan:
Till that which suits a part infects the whole,
And now is almost grown the habit of my soul.

VII

Hence, viper thoughts, that coil around my mind,
      Reality's dark dream!
I turn from you, and listen to the wind,
      Which long has raved unnoticed. What a scream
Of agony by torture lengthened out
That lute sent forth! Thou Wind, that rav'st without,
      Bare crag, or mountain-tairn, or blasted tree,
Or pine-grove whither woodman never clomb,
Or lonely house, long held the witches' home,
      Methinks were fitter instruments for thee,
Mad Lutanist! who in this month of showers,
Of dark-brown gardens, and of peeping flowers,
Mak'st Devils' yule, with worse than wintry song,
The blossoms, buds, and timorous leaves among.
      Thou Actor, perfect in all tragic sounds!
Thou mighty Poet, e'en to frenzy bold!
         What tell'st thou now about?
         'Tis of the rushing of an host in rout,
      With groans, of trampled men, with smarting wounds –
At once they groan with pain, and shudder with the cold!
But hush! there is a pause of deepest silence!
      And all that noise, as of a rushing crowd,
With groans, and tremulous shudderings – all is over –
      It tells another tale, with sounds less deep and loud!
         A tale of less affright,
         And tempered with delight,
As Otway's self had framed the tender lay, –

'Tis of a little child
Upon a lonesome wild,
Nor far from home, but she hath lost her way:
And now moans low in bitter grief and fear,
And now screams loud, and hopes to make her mother hear.

VIII

'Tis midnight, but small thoughts have I of sleep:
Full seldom may my friend such vigils keep!
Visit her, gentle Sleep! with wings of healing,
    And may this storm be but a mountain-birth,
May all the stars hang bright above her dwelling,
      Silent as though they watched the sleeping Earth!
       With light heart may she rise,
       Gay fancy, cheerful eyes,
Joy lift her spirit, joy attune her voice;
To her may all things live, from pole to pole,
   Their life the eddying of her living soul!
     O simple spirit, guided from above,
Dear Lady! friend devoutest of my choice,
Thus mayest thou ever, evermore rejoice.

– Kubla Khan (1816) –

In Xanadu did Kubla Khan
A stately pleasure-dome decree:
Where Alph, the sacred river, ran
Through caverns measureless to man
  Down to a sunless sea.
So twice five miles of fertile ground
With walls and towers were girdled round;
And there were gardens bright with sinuous rills,
Where blossomed many an incense-bearing tree;
And here were forests ancient as the hills,
Enfolding sunny spots of greenery.

But oh! that deep romantic chasm which slanted
Down the green hill athwart a cedarn cover!
A savage place! as holy and enchanted
As e'er beneath a waning moon was haunted
By woman wailing for her demon-lover!
And from this chasm, with ceaseless turmoil seething,
As if this earth in fast thick pants were breathing,
A mighty fountain momently was forced:
Amid whose swift half-intermitted burst
Huge fragments vaulted like rebounding hail,
Or chaffy grain beneath the thresher's flail:
And mid these dancing rocks at once and ever
It flung up momently the sacred river.
Five miles meandering with a mazy motion
Through wood and dale the sacred river ran,

Then reached the caverns measureless to man,
And sank in tumult to a lifeless ocean;
And 'mid this tumult Kubla heard from far
Ancestral voices prophesying war!
    The shadow of the dome of pleasure
    Floated midway on the waves;
    Where was heard the mingled measure
    From the fountain and the caves.
It was a miracle of rare device,
A sunny pleasure-dome with caves of ice!

    A damsel with a dulcimer
    In a vision once I saw:
    It was an Abyssinian maid
    And on her dulcimer she played,
    Singing of Mount Abora.
    Could I revive within me
    Her symphony and song,
    To such a deep delight 'twould win me,
That with music loud and long,
I would build that dome in air,
That sunny dome! those caves of ice!
And all who heard should see them there,
And all should cry, Beware! Beware!
His flashing eyes, his floating hair!
Weave a circle round him thrice,
And close your eyes with holy dread
For he on honey-dew hath fed,
And drunk the milk of Paradise.

– Work Without Hope (1825) –

All Nature seems at work. Slugs leave their lair –
The bees are stirring – birds are on the wing –
And Winter slumbering in the open air,
Wears on his smiling face a dream of Spring!
And I the while, the sole unbusy thing,
Nor honey make, nor pair, nor build, nor sing.

Yet well I ken the banks where amaranths blow,
Have traced the fount whence streams of nectar flow.
Bloom, O ye amaranths! bloom for whom ye may,
For me ye bloom not! Glide, rich streams, away!
With lips unbrightened, wreathless brow, I stroll:
And would you learn the spells that drowse my soul?
Work without Hope draws nectar in a sieve,
And Hope without an object cannot live.

– The Knight's Tomb (1834) –

Where is the grave of Sir Arthur O'Kellyn?
Where may the grave of that good man be? –
By the side of a spring, on the breast of Helvellyn,
Under the twigs of a young birch tree!
The oak that in summer was sweet to hear,
And rustled its leaves in the fall of the year,
And whistled and roared in the winter alone,
Is gone, – and the birch in its stead is grown. –
The Knight's bones are dust,
And his good sword rust; –
His soul is with the saints, I trust.

ROBERT SOUTHEY
(1774–1843)

T he son of a bankrupt linen-draper, Robert Southey
was born in Bristol and was educated at Westminster
School and Balliol College, Oxford, which he left without
taking a degree. He published his first collection of poems,
called *Poems*, in 1795 and in 1813 he became Poet Laureate,
a post he held until his death. Southey was a prolific and
influential poet, essayist, historian, travel writer, biographer,
translator and polemicist. His work often explored histori-
cal and mythological themes, drawing inspiration from clas-
sical literature and medieval romances through epic poems,
ballads and prose writings. His essays, histories and reviews
tackled the issues confronting a period dominated by imperi-
alism and industrialisation and his biographies, including the
best-selling *The Life of Horatio Nelson, Lord Viscount* (1813),
contributed to the formation of the celebrity culture we rec-
ognise today. Although Southey's popularity has perhaps
waned, his influence on the development of Romantic poetry
remains significant and his work provides a valuable window
into the literary and intellectual currents of his time. Southey
and his wife Edith Fricker (whose sister, Sara, married Col-
eridge) moved to Keswick in 1803 after the death of their first
child. They lived at Greta Hall, which they initially shared
with Coleridge's family, and Southey's fame brought visitors
from across the world to the town. He died in Keswick and
is buried in the churchyard of Crosthwaite Church, where he
had worshipped for forty years. There is a memorial to him
inside the church, with an epitaph written by Wordsworth.

– Ode, Written on the First of December
(1795) –

Tho' now no more the musing ear
Delights to listen to the breeze
That lingers o'er the green wood shade,
I love thee Winter! well.

Sweet are the harmonies of Spring,
Sweet is the summer's evening gale,
Pleasant the autumnal winds that shake
The many-colour'd grove.

And pleasant to the sober'd soul
The silence of the wintry scene,
When Nature shrouds her in her trance

Not undelightful now to roam
The wild heath sparkling on the sight;
Not undelightful now to pace
The forest's ample rounds;

And see the spangled branches shine,
And mark the moss of many a hue
That varies the old tree's brown bark,
Or o'er the grey stone spreads.

The cluster'd berries claim the eye
O'er the bright hollies gay green leaves,
The ivy round the leafless oak
Clasps its full foliage close.

So VIRTUE diffident of strength
Clings to RELIGION's firmer aid,
And by RELIGION's aid upheld
Endures calamity.

Nor void of beauties now the spring,
Whose waters hid from summer sun
Have sooth'd the thirsty pilgrim's ear
With more than melody.

The green moss shines with icey glare,
The long grass bends its spear-like form,
And lovely is the silvery scene
When faint the sunbeams smile.

Reflection too may love the hour
When Nature, hid in Winter's grave,
No more expands the bursting bud
Or bids the flowret bloom.

For Nature soon in Spring's best charms
Shall rise reviv'd from Winter's grave.
Again expand the bursting bud,
And bid the flowret bloom.

– The Battle of Blenheim (1798) –

It was a summer evening,
　Old Kaspar's work was done,
And he before his cottage door
　Was sitting in the sun,
And by him sported on the green
　His little grandchild Wilhelmine.

She saw her brother Peterkin
　Roll something large and round,
Which he beside the rivulet
　In playing there had found;
He came to ask what he had found,
　That was so large, and smooth, and round.

Old Kaspar took it from the boy,
　Who stood expectant by;
And then the old man shook his head,
　And, with a natural sigh,
''Tis some poor fellow's skull,' said he,
　'Who fell in the great victory.

'I find them in the garden,
　For there's many here about;
And often when I go to plough,
　The ploughshare turns them out!
For many thousand men,' said he,
　'Were slain in that great victory.'

'Now tell us what 'twas all about,'
    Young Peterkin, he cries;
And little Wilhelmine looks up
    With wonder-waiting eyes;
'Now tell us all about the war,
    And what they fought each other for.'

'It was the English,' Kaspar cried,
    'Who put the French to rout;
But what they fought each other for,
    I could not well make out;
But everybody said,' quoth he,
    'That 'twas a famous victory.

'My father lived at Blenheim then,
    Yon little stream hard by;
They burnt his dwelling to the ground,
    And he was forced to fly;
So with his wife and child he fled,
    Nor had he where to rest his head.

'With fire and sword the country round
    Was wasted far and wide,
And many a childing mother then,
    And new-born baby died; ·
But things like that, you know, must be
    At every famous victory.

'They say it was a shocking sight
   After the field was won;
For many thousand bodies here
   Lay rotting in the sun;
But things like that, you know, must be
   After a famous victory.

'Great praise the Duke of Marlbro' won,
   And our good Prince Eugene.'
'Why, 'twas a very wicked thing!'
   Said little Wilhelmine.
'Nay . . . nay . . . my little girl,' quoth he,
   'It was a famous victory.

'And everybody praised the Duke
   Who this great fight did win.'
'But what good came of it at last?'
   Quoth little Peterkin.
'Why that I cannot tell,' said he,
   'But 'twas a famous victory.'

– The Cataract of Lodore (1820) –

      'How does the water
      Come down at Lodore?'
      My little boy asked me
      Thus, once on a time;
      And moreover he tasked me

118

To tell him in rhyme.
Anon, at the word,
There first came one daughter,
And then came another,
To second and third
The request of their brother,
And to hear how the water
Comes down at Lodore,
With its rush and its roar,
As many a time
They had seen it before.
So I told them in rhyme,
For of rhymes I had store;
And 'twas in my vocation
For their recreation
That so I should sing;
Because I was Laureate
To them and the King.

From its sources which well
In the tarn on the fell;
From its fountains
In the mountains,
Its rills and its gills;
Through moss and through brake,
It runs and it creeps
For a while, till it sleeps
In its own little lake.
And thence at departing,

Awakening and starting,
It runs through the reeds,
And away it proceeds,
Through meadow and glade,
In sun and in shade,
And through the wood-shelter,
Among crags in its flurry,
Helter-skelter,
Hurry-skurry.
Here it comes sparkling,
And there it lies darkling;
Now smoking and frothing
Its tumult and wrath in,
Till, in this rapid race
On which it is bent,
It reaches the place
Of its steep descent.

The cataract strong
Then plunges along,
Striking and raging

As if a war raging
Its caverns and rocks among;
Rising and leaping,
Sinking and creeping,
Swelling and sweeping,
Showering and springing,
Flying and flinging,
Writhing and ringing,

Eddying and whisking,
Spouting and frisking,
Turning and twisting,
Around and around
With endless rebound:
Smiting and fighting,
A sight to delight in;
Confounding, astounding,
Dizzying and deafening the ear with its sound.

Collecting, projecting,
Receding and speeding,
And shocking and rocking,
And darting and parting,
And threading and spreading,
And whizzing and hissing,
And dripping and skipping,
And hitting and splitting,
And shining and twining,
And rattling and battling,
And shaking and quaking,
And pouring and roaring,
And waving and raving,
And tossing and crossing,
And flowing and going,
And running and stunning,
And foaming and roaming,
And dinning and spinning,
And dropping and hopping,

And working and jerking,
And guggling and struggling,
And heaving and cleaving,
And moaning and groaning;
And glittering and frittering,
And gathering and feathering,
And whitening and brightening,
And quivering and shivering,
And hurrying and skurrying,
And thundering and floundering;

Dividing and gliding and sliding,
And falling and brawling and sprawling,
And driving and riving and striving,
And sprinkling and twinkling and wrinkling,
And sounding and bounding and rounding,
And bubbling and troubling and doubling,
And grumbling and rumbling and tumbling,
And clattering and battering and shattering;

Retreating and beating and meeting and sheeting,
Delaying and straying and playing and spraying,
Advancing and prancing and glancing and dancing,
Recoiling, turmoiling and toiling and boiling,
And gleaming and streaming and steaming and beaming,
And rushing and flushing and brushing and gushing,
And flapping and rapping and clapping and slapping,
And curling and whirling and purling and twirling,
And thumping and plumping and bumping and jumping,
And dashing and flashing and splashing and clashing;

And so never ending, but always descending,
Sounds and motions for ever and ever are blending
All at once and all o'er, with a mighty uproar;
And this way the water comes down at Lodore.

– The Holly-Tree (1823) –

O reader! hast thou ever stood to see
The Holly-tree?
The eye that contemplates it well perceives
Its glossy leaves
Ordered by an Intelligence so wise
As might confound the Atheist's sophistries.

Below, a circling fence, its leaves are seen,
Wrinkled and keen;

No grazing cattle, through their prickly round,
Can reach to wound;
But, as they grow where nothing is to fear,
Smooth and unarmed the pointless leaves appear.

I love to view these things with curious eyes,
And moralize;
And in this wisdom of the Holly-tree
Can emblem see
Wherewith, perchance, to make a pleasant rhyme, –
One which may profit in the after-time.

Thus, though abroad, perchance, I might appear
Harsh and austere;
To those who on my leisure would intrude,
Reserved and rude;
Gentle at home amid my friends I'd be,
Like the high leaves upon the Holly-tree.

And should my youth – as youth is apt, I know, –
Some harshness show,
All vain asperities I, day by day,
Would wear away,
Till the smooth temper of my age should be
Like the high leaves upon the Holly-tree.

And as, when all the summer trees are seen
So bright and green,
The Holly-leaves their fadeless hues display
Less bright than they;
But when the bare and wintry woods we see,
What then so cheerful as the Holly-tree? –

So, serious should my youth appear among
The thoughtless throng;
So would I seem, amid the young and gay,
More grave than they;
That in my age as cheerful I might be
As the green winter of the Holly-tree.

CHARLES LAMB

(1775–1834)

Charles Lamb was an English essayist, poet and anti-
quarian, best known for his hugely popular *Essays of
Elia* and for the children's book *Tales from Shakespeare*, co-
authored with his sister, Mary Lamb. Born in London, Lamb
was the son of a clerk and the youngest of seven children.
The family was ambitious for its two sons and was success-
ful in entering Lamb at Christ's Hospital, a London charity
school of merit. There he met Coleridge, who introduced
Lamb to Wordsworth and who helped stir his growing inter-
est in poetry. Lamb left school early because he had a severe
stutter and found work as a clerk at the South Sea House
and later at the East India Company, where he remained
for thirty-three years while pursuing his literary interests.
In 1776, during a fit of 'lunacy', Mary Lamb stabbed their
mother to death. Rather than leave her in an asylum, Lamb
persuaded the court to release her into his care. There was,
perhaps, no writer with a wider circle of literary friends than
Charles Lamb. While Lamb is mostly known as an essayist,
his association with Coleridge and Wordsworth left a deep
impression on his work, which is characteristically 'Romantic'
in that it evokes a feeling, a particular character or moment
of experience not so much for an intellectual purpose as for
endowing their own loves with heightened vividness. Lamb
visited Coleridge and Wordsworth in the Lake District and
was inspired by its natural beauty, but claimed he could never
live away from London.

– A Vision of Repentance (1797) –

I saw a famous fountain, in my dream,
  Where shady pathways to a valley led;
A weeping willow lay upon that stream,
  And all around the fountain brink were spread
Wide-branching trees, with dark green leaf rich clad,
Forming a doubtful twilight – desolate and sad.

The place was such, that whoso enter'd in,
  Disrobèd was of every earthly thought,
And straight became as one that knew not sin,
  Or to the world's first innocence was brought;
Enseem'd it now, he stood on holy ground,
In sweet and tender melancholy wrapt around.

A most strange calm stole o'er my soothèd sprite;
  Long time I stood, and longer had I staid,
When, lo! I saw, saw by the sweet moonlight,
  Which came in silence o'er that silent shade,
Where, near the fountain, SOMETHING like DESPAIR
Made, of that weeping-willow, garlands for her hair.
And eke with painful fingers she inwove
  Many an uncouth stem of savage thorn –
'The willow garland, *that* was for her love,
  And *these* her bleeding temples would adorn.'
With sighs her heart nigh burst, salt tears fast fell,
As mournfully she bended o'er that sacred well.

To whom when I addrest myself to speak,
  She lifted up her eyes, and nothing said;
The delicate red came mantling o'er her cheek,
  And, gath'ring up her loose attire, she fled
To the dark covert of that woody shade,
And in her goings seem'd a timid gentle maid.

Revolving in my mind what this should mean,
  And why that lovely lady plainèd so;
Perplex'd in thought at that mysterious scene,
  And doubting if 'twere best to stay or go,
I cast mine eyes in wistful gaze around,
When from the shades came slow a small and
    plaintive sound.

    'Psyche am I, who love to dwell
    In these brown shades, this woody dell,
    Where never busy mortal came,
    Till now, to pry upon my shame.

    At thy feet what thou dost see
    The waters of repentance be,
    Which, night and day, I must augment
    With tears, like a true penitent,
    If haply so my day of grace
    Be not yet past; and this lone place,
    O'er-shadowy, dark, excludeth hence
    All thoughts but grief and penitence.'

    'Why dost thou weep, thou gentle maid!
    And wherefore in this barren shade

Thy hidden thoughts with sorrow feed?
Can thing so fair repentance need?'

'O! I have done a deed of shame,
And tainted is my virgin fame,
And stain'd the beauteous maiden white,
In which my bridal robes were dight.'

'And who the promised spouse, declare:
And what those bridal garments were.'

'Severe and saintly righteousness
Compos'd the clear white bridal dress;
JESUS, the son of Heaven's high king,
Bought with his blood the marriage ring.
'A wretched sinful creature, I
Deem'd lightly of that sacred tie,
Gave to a treacherous WORLD my heart,
And play'd the foolish wanton's part.

Soon to these murky shades I came,
To hide from the sun's light my shame.
And still I haunt this woody dell,
And bathe me in that healing well,
Whose waters clear have influence
From sin's foul stains the soul to cleanse;
And, night and day, I them augment,
With tears, like a true penitent,
Until, due expiation made,
And fit atonement fully paid,
The Lord and Bridegroom me present,

Where in sweet strains of high consent,
God's throne before, the Seraphim
Shall chaunt the extatic marriage hymn.'

'Now Christ restore thee soon' – I said,
And thenceforth all my dream was fled.

– The Old Familiar Faces (1798) –

I have had playmates, I have had companions,
In my days of childhood, in my joyful school-days,
All, all are gone, the old familiar faces.

I have been laughing, I have been carousing,
Drinking late, sitting late, with my bosom cronies,
All, all are gone, the old familiar faces.

I loved a love once, fairest among women;
Closed are her doors on me, I must not see her –
All, all are gone, the old familiar faces.

I have a friend, a kinder friend has no man;
Like an ingrate, I left my friend abruptly;
Left him, to muse on the old familiar faces.

Ghost-like, I paced round the haunts of my childhood.
Earth seemed a desert I was bound to traverse,
Seeking to find the old familiar faces.

Friend of my bosom, thou more than a brother,
Why wert not thou born in my father's dwelling?
So might we talk of the old familiar faces –

How some they have died, and some they have left me,
And some are taken from me; all are departed;
All, all are gone, the old familiar faces.

– Letter to Thomas Manning, 24 September,
1802 –

My Dear Manning,

Since the date of my last letter, I have been a traveller, A strong desire seized me of visiting remote regions. My first impulse was to go and see Paris. It was a trivial objection to my aspiring mind that I did not understand a word of the language, since I certainly intend some time in my life to see Paris, and equally certainly never intend to learn the language; therefore that could be no objection. However, I am very glad I did not go, because you had left Paris (I see) before I could have set out. I believe Stoddart promising to go with me another year prevented that plan. My next scheme (for to my restless, ambitious mind London was become a bed of thorns) was to visit the far-famed peak in Derbyshire, where the Devil sits, they say, without breeches. This my purer mind rejected as indelicate. And my final resolve was a tour to the Lakes. I set out with Mary to Keswick, without giving Coleridge any notice; for my time, being precious, did not admit of it. He received us with all the hospitality in the world, and gave up his time to show us all the wonders of the country. He dwells upon a small hill by the side of Keswick, in a comfortable house, quite enveloped on all sides by a net of mountains: great floundering bears and monsters they seemed, all couchant and asleep. We got in in the evening, travelling in a post-chaise from Penrith, in the midst of a gorgeous sunshine, which transmuted all the mountains into colours, purple, etc. We thought we had got into fairy-land. But that went off (as it never came again; while we stayed, we had no more fine sunsets); and we entered Coleridge's comfortable study just in the dusk, when the mountains were all dark, with clouds upon their heads. Such an impression I never received from objects of sight before, nor do I suppose that I can ever again. Glorious creatures, fine old fellows, Skiddaw, etc. I never shall forget ye, how ye lay about that night, like an intrenchment; gone to bed, as it seemed for the night, but promising that ye were to be seen in the morning. Coleridge had got a blazing fire in his study, which is a large, antique, ill-shaped room, with an old-fashioned organ, never played upon, big enough for a church, shelves of scattered folios, an Æolian harp, and an old sofa, half-bed, etc.; and all looking out upon the last fading view of Skiddaw and his broad-breasted brethren. What a night! Here we stayed three full weeks, in which time I visited Wordsworth's cottage, where we stayed a day or two with the Clarksons (good people and most hospitable, at whose house we tarried one day and night), and saw Lloyd. The Wordsworths were gone to Calais. They have since been in London, and passed much time with us; he has now gone into Yorkshire to be married. So we have seen Keswick, Grasmere, Ambleside, Ulswater (where the Clarksons live), and a place at the other end of Ulswater – I forget the name – to which we travelled on a very sultry day, over the middle of Helvellyn. We have clambered up to the top of Skiddaw, and I have waded up the bed of Lodore. In fine, I have satisfied myself that there is such a thing as that which tourists call romantic, which I very much suspected before; they make such a spluttering about it, and toss their splendid epithets around them, till they give as dim a light as at four o'clock next morning the lamps do after an illumination. Mary was excessively tired when she got about half way up Skiddaw; but we came to a cold rill (than which nothing can be imagined more cold, running over cold stones), and with the reinforcement of a draught of cold water she surmounted it most manfully. Oh, its fine black head, and the bleak air atop of it, with a prospect of mountains all about and about, making you giddy; and then Scotland afar off, and the border countries so famous in song and ballad! It was a day that will stand out like a mountain, I am sure, in my life. But I am returned (I have now been come home near three weeks; I was a month out), and you cannot conceive the degradation I felt at first, from being accustomed to wander free as air among mountains, and bathe in rivers without being controlled by any one, to come home and work. I felt very little. I had been dreaming I was a very great man. But that is going off, and I find I shall conform in time to that state of life to which it has pleased God to call me. Besides, after all, Fleet Street and the Strand are better places to live in for good and all than amidst Skiddaw. Still, I turn back to those great places where I wandered about, participating in their greatness. After all, I could not live in Skiddaw. I could spend a year – two, three years among them; but I must have a prospect of seeing Fleet Street at the end of that time, or I should mope and pine away, I know. Still, Skiddaw is a fine creature.

– Thoughtless Cruelty (1809) –

There, Robert, you have kill'd that fly –
And should you thousand ages try
The life you've taken to supply,
You could not do it.

You surely must have been devoid
Of thought and sense, to have destroy'd
A thing which no way you annoy'd –
You'll one day rue it.

Twas but a fly perhaps you'll say,
That's born in April, dies in May;
That does but just learn to display
His wings one minute,

And in the next is vanish'd quite.
A bird devours it in his flight –
Or come a cold blast in the night,
There's no breath in it.

The bird but seeks his proper food –
And Providence, whose power endu'd
That fly with life, when it thinks good,
May justly take it.

But you have no excuses for't –
A life by Nature made so short,
Less reason is that you for sport
Should shorter make it.

A fly a little thing you rate –
But, Robert do not estimate
A creature's pain by small or great;
The greatest being

Can have but fibres, nerves, and flesh,
And these the smallest ones possess,
Although their frame and structure less
Escape our seeing.

– The First Leaf of Spring (1832) –

Thou fragile, filmy, gossamery thing,
First leaf of spring!
At every lightest breath that quakest,
And with a zephyr shakest;
Scarce stout enough to hold thy slender form together
In calmest halcyon weather:
Next sister to the web that spiders weave,
Poor flutterers to deceive
Into their treacherous silken bed:
O! how art thou sustained, how nourished!
All trivial as thou art,
Without dispute,
Thou play'st a mighty part;
And art the herald to a throng
Of buds, blooms, fruit,

That shall thy cracking branches sway,
While birds on every spray
Shall pay the copious fruitage with a sylvan song.
So 'tis with thee, whoe'er on thee shall look,
First leaf of this beginning modest book.
Slender thou art, God knowest,
And little grace bestowest,
But in thy train shall follow after,
Wit, wisdom, seriousness, in hand with laughter;
Provoking jests, restraining soberness,
In their appropriate dress;
And I shall joy to be outdone
By those who brighter trophies won,
Without a grief,
That I thy slender promise have begun,
First leaf.

Other titles from Notting Hill Editions*

Essays on the Self
Virginia Woolf
Introduced by Joanna Kavenna

In these essays Virginia Woolf explores the nature of the finite self ('Who am I?' 'Who is everybody else?') and how individual experience might be relayed. Each of us exists once on earth, each one of us speaks of 'myself' and 'yourself', distinguishing the lone self from a bewildering array of other selves. How to express the perceptions of this self? Trust yourself, Woolf suggests, live within the beauty and strangeness of ordinary life.

Beautiful and Impossible Things: Selected Essays of Oscar Wilde
Introduced by Gyles Brandreth

This selection of Oscar Wilde's writing provides a fresh perspective on his character and thinking. Compiled from his lecture tours, newspaper articles, essays and epigrams, these pieces show that beneath the trademark wit, Wilde was a deeply humane and visionary writer, as challenging today as he was in the late 1800s. This edition includes essays on interior design, prison reform, Shakespeare, the dramatic dialogue *Decay of Lying* and the seminal *Soul of Man*.

A Strange Life: Selected Essays of Louisa May Alcott
Edited by Liz Rosenberg with a Preface by Jane Smiley

Louisa May Alcott is best known as the author of *Little Women*. But she was also a noted essayist who wrote on a wide range of subjects, including her father's failed utopian commune, life as a Civil War nurse and her experience as a young woman sent to work in service to alleviate her family's poverty. Blending gentle satire with reportage and emotive biography, *A Strange Life* – edited by Liz Rosenberg and with a preface by Jane Smiley – shows Alcott to be one of the sharpest wits in American literature.

Happy Half-Hours: Selected Writings of A. A. Milne
Introduced by Frank Cotterell-Boyce

A delightful selection of articles by the ever-popular A. A. Milne, many of which haven't been in print for decades. Milne had a talent for regularly turning out a thousand whimsical words on lost hats and umbrellas, golf, married life, cheap cigars, and any amount of life's other little difficulties. It also includes some of his fiercely argued writings on pacifism. Introduced by the prize-winning children's author and Waterstones Children's Laureate 2024–2026 Frank Cottrell-Boyce, this volume features the very best of A. A. Milne in one delightful volume.

On Cats: An Anthology
Introduced by Margaret Atwood

Introduced by Margaret Atwood, who was a 'cat-deprived young child', the writers in these pages reflect on the curious feline qualities that inspire devotion in their owners, even when it seems one-sided. Includes contributions from Doris Lessing, Edward Gorey, Mary Gaitskill, Ernest Hemingway, Caitlin Moran, Nikola Tesla, Muriel Spark, John Keats, Lynne Truss, Guy du Maupassant, Rebecca West, Hillarie Belloc and more.

On Dogs: An Anthology
Introduced by Tracey Ullman

Introduced by Tracey Ullman (an inveterate adopter of strays), this beautifully illustrated anthology traces the canine's extraordinary journey from working animal to pampered pet. Includes contributions from Shakespeare, Alice Walker, James Thurber, Miranda Hart, Will Self, J. M. Barrie, Jack London, A. A. Gill, Brigitte Bardot, John Steinbeck, David Sedaris, J. R. Ackerley, Virginia Woolf and more.

*All titles are available in the UK, and some titles are available in the rest of the world. For more information please visit www.nottinghilleditions.com.

A selection of our titles is distributed in the US and Canada by New York Review Books. For more information on available titles please visit www.nyrb.com